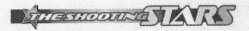

The Big Fudge

GW00802261

Watch out for other titles in The Shooting Stars series:

✴

The Green-eyed Monster ✴
✴ Maddy's Big Break
The Stage Kiss
Lights . . . Camera . . . Ghost!
Understudy to Miss Perfect

✴

LEXILE™ 720

Scholastic Press
345 Pacific Highway
Lindfield NSW 2070
an imprint of Scholastic Australia Pty Limited (ABN 11 000 614 577)
PO Box 579
Gosford NSW 2250
www.scholastic.com.au

Part of the Scholastic Group
Sydney ● Auckland ● New York ● Toronto ● London ● Mexico City
● New Delhi ● Hong Kong ● Buenos Aires ● Puerto Rico

First published in 2002.
Text copyright © Tempany Deckert, 2002.
Cover illustrations copyright © Scholastic Australia, 2002.
Cover photos by Joseph Saw, Sydney.
Cover design by Ark Publishing, Black Rock, Victoria.

National Library of Australia Cataloguing-in-publications entry
    Deckert, Tempany, 1978–.
    The big fudge
    ISBN 1 86504 400 8.
    I. Teenage girls—Juvenile fiction. 2. Bands (Music)—Juvenile
    fiction. 3. Teenage actors—Juvenile fiction. I. Title.
    (Series: The shooting stars (Sydney, N.S.W.); 6).
A823.4

Typeset in Galliard.

Printed by McPherson's Printing Group, Maryborough, Vic.

10 9 8 7 6 5 4 3 2 1   2 3 4 5 6 / 0

The Big Fudge

by Tempany Deckert

A Scholastic Press
book
from
Scholastic Australia

chapter one

I made myself go cross-eyed. It meant that when I looked at the girls sitting near me, they almost looked like my friends, Louie, Tahnee and Dene, in a blurry kind of way. I desperately wished my best friends went to school with me. When I'm with them, I actually feel like someone. When I'm at school, I feel like no-one even knows or cares who I am. I imagined Tahnee was pulling faces at the teacher and Louie was braiding my hair.

Suddenly, the hairs on the back of my neck stood up. Somewhere, someone in the room was staring at me. I could feel it. I knew there was probably only one person who would be staring at me and it wasn't because she wanted to have a girly chat.

Nina Karter's eyes could've bored a hole in my head. I didn't care. There was no way I was going to turn around and help her out for the twenty-third time this term. Yes, I was keeping count.

'Maddy, I'm talking to you. What's the answer for number eight?'

I kept my head down and remained silent. I

was not going to turn around. I, Maddy Wilkinson, was not going to help her out again. One hundred percent negative.

I couldn't believe I'd been so naïve. At the start of the year I had deliberately chosen all the same subjects as Nina, the cool girl in our year, in the hope that we would be in the same classes. I'd deduced that if I hung around her more, I too, would become cool. But it seemed like there was more chance of my goldfish, Leo, growing legs, than there was of me becoming cool.

'Maddy? Helloooo? Anyone home?' Nina whispered loudly.

Foolishly, I glanced back at her and her big blue eyes and shiny brown hair. How did she get her hair that shiny? It was like something out of a shampoo commercial.

'Finally. I've been calling you for ages,' she whined. 'What's the answer to number eight?'

The cool girl of our year only ever spoke to me for two reasons: when she needed an answer in a maths exam or when she felt like humiliating me in front of the whole class. Luckily, today's conversation only involved maths. Unless, of course, the humiliating bit was yet to come.

'One hundred and twenty-three,' I decided to admit. Who knew what Nina would put me through if I didn't give her the answer. Hopefully, now she would leave me alone.

'OK, kids, time's up. Please hand your papers to the front and pack up your things,' said our teacher, Mr Winfrey.

I packed up slowly, deliberately hanging back while Nina grabbed her books and sauntered out into the corridor. I breathed a sigh of relief. A whole lesson without humiliation was a rare occurrence. I picked up my own books and headed for the lockers.

Nina's locker was at the opposite end of the corridor to mine, so I calculated that by the time I left the classroom she would be well out of my way. No such luck. There she was, standing smack bang in the middle of the corridor, surrounded by every girl in our class.

'How many of you think you can make it to my birthday party?' she asked the adoring crowd.

What birthday party? I hadn't heard anything about a birthday party. Once again, I was the last girl in class to hear about things. It wasn't a big surprise but I was still annoyed. Surely one of them could've told me?

'Hands up everyone who can come,' Nina demanded. All the girls' hands shot up in the air eagerly. Nina smiled. 'That's fantastic! Unfortunately, though, Dad said I can only invite five of you, so, Darla, Melissa, Melanie, Chloe and um, let's see . . .' Nina deliberately hesitated in her final pick to make the unchosen ones plead and beg.

It was pathetic. '. . . and Kathy. Great. We are going to have the best time!'

The unchosen slunk away and made a big enough gap to let me pass. I couldn't believe I was the only girl she hadn't told. Normally at least a couple of us were left out.

'Oh, Maddy,' Nina said to me as I tried to edge past her. 'I forgot to tell you. It's my birthday this weekend and my dad is organising the most stupendous party.'

I couldn't believe it. Was Nina Karter about to invite *me* to her birthday party? Maybe I'd become cool without even knowing it.

'But as it's costing Dad a fortune, he's restricted the invitation list to only five girls. Sorry about that.' Every word sounded sincere but there was a look in Nina's eyes that gave her meanness away.

I said nothing and headed off. That's the rule my friend, Dene, taught me: if you can't say anything nice, don't say anything. But you're allowed to think the nastiest thoughts you want. Dene swears that it makes you feel better.

Nina Karter has bad hair . . . no, she had nice hair. Nina Karter wears gross clothes . . . no, she had the funkiest clothes of any girl I'd ever met. Nina Karter is stupid . . . well, she wasn't the smartest but she wasn't really stupid.

The whole nasty thought thing just wasn't

working for me. All of a sudden, I thought of one. Nina Karter is mean. There. That *was* true. Dene would be proud of me.

'Now that the losers have gone, I can tell you what we're doing for the party,' Nina said, thinking that I was out of earshot. Losers? We were not losers! 'Dad has managed to scam tickets to a concert featuring . . . wait for it . . . TEA SERVICE!' she squealed.

The chosen ones jumped up and down and hugged vomitus Nina. As much as I hated to admit it, that *was* cool. Tea Service was my favourite band.

I reached my locker and angrily shoved my maths book inside. How dare she call me a loser! I wasn't a loser. I didn't have the nicest clothes and I wasn't the prettiest girl at school, but that didn't make me a loser. The fact that my parents were forcing me to get a plate to fix my teeth was a bit dorky, I guess, but not loserish. Fair enough, I could admit to not being cool but I certainly was *not* a loser!

And how had Nina's dad got her tickets to a Tea Service concert? Tea Service was completely sold out. My best friends and I had queued for hours only to be told that every single ticket had been bought.

I had to get home immediately and tell the gang about it. I see Tahnee, Dene and Louise, my best friends, every Tuesday evening for our acting class at The Shooting Stars, and we nearly always hang out on the weekends. As you can imagine, not having your best friends at school means you spend a lot of time on the phone and the internet. I couldn't wait to tell them about vomitus Nina and her Tea Service birthday party. They wouldn't believe it.

I grabbed the stuff I needed for homework and shoved it into my backpack. At the back of my locker sat my fluorescent bicycle outfit in a crumpled ball. My parents make me wear it when I ride my bike home, as a safety precaution. I pulled it out, hid it under my arm and walked to the toilets. Inside a cubicle, I quickly slipped the ugly jacket and pants over my clothes. I stuck my head out of the cubicle to see if anyone else was in the bathroom. As usual, the end of the day was not a popular time to go to the toilet. The coast was clear. I pulled my helmet out of my backpack and made a run for it. As I ran past the bathroom mirrors, I caught a glimpse of myself. I froze in front of my reflection. There I was, covered from head to toe in fluorescent yellow. How many other kids at school wore fluorescent outfits to ride their bikes home? None. Suddenly it hit me. Maybe Nina was right. Maybe I was a loser.

'Maddy! You are not a loser. I swear to goddessness,' pleaded my best friend, Louie.

'Louise Eary, you don't have to protect me. It's too late. I know I'm a loser. I have gross clothes, a boring haircut, I'm not that funny, I wear a clown outfit to ride my bike home, tomorrow I have to get an ugly plate from the orthodontist and I'm good at maths. There is no hiding the truth that I am a big, uncool, loser dork. If I was as popular as you say I am, then why didn't Nina invite me to her party?'

Louie sighed. Our phone conversation had been going for a while. There was nothing she could say to make me change my mind about my rank in teenage society.

'OK, fine, you think you're a big loser dork. Fair enough. But do you really think a five star teenager such as myself would choose a loser dork as her best friend?' she argued. It was a good point.

'Maybe you're a dork as well,' I joked. Talking to Louie was making me feel better. Not only was my best friend good at debating, she constantly made me and our other friends at drama school do improvisations as lawyers. If anyone was going to talk me out of this, Louie was. 'OK, well let's say I'm not a loser. I know I'm still uncool compared to Nina Karter.'

'What!' Louie yelled. 'You don't even like Nina Karter. You said she's mean, rude and a snob. Why do you suddenly want to be like her?'

'Because everyone likes her, that's why. I want

to be the girl that everyone follows down the corridor for once.' I twirled the phone cord around my finger and stared at a mouldy peach in the bottom of the fruit bowl. I understood what Louie was saying but it didn't make any difference. Lou couldn't know how I felt as she'd never been a dork. She'd always been one of the cool kids with her funky clothes, bizarre house and easy-going parents.

'Maddy, you're doing a Mrs Hannigan, aren't you?' My friends and I at drama school have our own secret language. 'Doing a Mrs Hannigan' means you feel like you are going crazy. 'Well, you can stop it right now. There is no way you are uncool.' Louie's voice had changed into the serious well-spoken tone that she only used when she pretended to be a lawyer. I was about to hear her closing argument. 'You are an incredible singer whose work is on the radio all the time.'

'What? My jingles? They don't really count,' I argued.

'Maddy! Don't interrupt. You go to drama school and are always auditioning for really amazing shows and plays. You have your own rehearsal room at your house and your very own goldfish. You don't have any brothers or sisters that you have to share stuff with and you're incredibly clever. That, to me, sounds like a pretty interesting and cool person.'

I reminded Louie about our drama school dance where I did a very good impression of a statue. I didn't move for the whole night. 'I was the only girl who didn't get asked to dance because everyone knows what an unco I am. I stood in the corner and was bored out of my mind the whole time.'

'That's rubbish! You did get asked; you refused to dance, remember?'

Hmm, Louie was right.

'But that's only because I know what an unco I am. Have you ever noticed that all cool people can dance?'

Another huge sigh came down the phone. 'Fine. Why don't you go ask your dice if you are cool or not, then. I bet they say you are the coolest of the cool.'

'No, I can't. I'm giving the dice up. Only dorks play games based on maths.' I used to play this probability game that would give me yes or no answers to questions I wasn't sure about. Everyone kept telling me it didn't work and that it was stupid. They were obviously right, so I had thrown the dice away and sworn that I would never touch them ever again.

'You've given the dice up? I can't believe it. Tahnee and Meano Deno aren't going to believe this. I'm going to send them an e-mail about it.'

'Make sure you tell them about Nina getting

tickets to Tea Service, too. If Nina's dad can get tickets, then I'm sure Deno and Tahnee can get them.'

'Good thinking, Madds.'

Tahnee Caruso is the funniest girl Louie and I have ever met. She is also incredible at imitating people's voices and pulling off practical jokes and scams. If anyone could find some Tea Service tickets floating around, Tahnee could. Deno, on the other hand, is tall, beautiful and straight to the point. She's not afraid of anyone or anything and she'll say whatever she's thinking. Together they make a great team for finding things out.

'So tell me, Madds, who's your favourite Tea Service band member and why?'

'Hmm. I think, I'd have to say Nick Geoffries because he's such a good singer.'

'Maddy! You always do that. Why can't you just say it's because he's the cutest?' Louie was trying to make me embarrassed. She knows how funny I can get about boys. Nick Geoffries was really cute. He even looks a bit like this guy I have a crush on at drama school, called Jason.

'Hey!' shouted Louie. 'I've thought of something to make you feel cool!'

Louise Eary proceeded to give me the instructions to Operation Groove. It sounded completely stupid but she was convinced I would feel like a different teenager afterwards.

'I don't know about this, Louie. It sounds pretty silly.'

'Trust me, it'll work. Hey, I've got to do my homework and send some e-mails so I'd better get off the phone. Good luck with the dentist tomorrow. I'm sure it won't be as bad as you think.'

'Hmm, hope so. Thanks, Lou. I'll see you in drama class tomorrow night.' I hung up the phone and looked at the instructions I'd copied down. There was no way it was going to work.

'Maddy, can you set the table? Dinner's ready,' Mum said. I decided to leave Operation Groove till the morning. I placed the instructions in my pocket and went to collect the cutlery.

One of Tea Service's songs came into my head as I laid the knives and forks around the table: *She steals my socks, she eats my food, she pays no rent and is always rude.* The girl in the song sounded like rude Nina. Selfish, insensitive and mean. I couldn't believe she was going to see them in concert and I wasn't. How had her dad got tickets? I tried to forget about it. Tahnee and Deno would solve the problem.

chapter two

I had my eyes screwed shut and I was willing myself to fall asleep. But it was no use. In the distance I could faintly hear some birds chirping. I lay there, imagining what kind of bird made chirps like that, when it dawned on me. It was almost daytime! I sat up and looked at my alarm clock. It was nearly six in the morning! Finally, I could get up.

For almost a year now I've had trouble getting to sleep. It's really annoying, unless Tahnee is having trouble sleeping as well and sends me e-mails and jokes to keep us entertained.

I didn't have to get to the dentist until nine o'clock so I had enough time to put Operation Groove into action. I changed out of my pyjamas into jeans and my favourite red T-shirt that Louie gave me for my birthday. I tied my hair back in a ponytail and retrieved the list from my pocket.

STEP ONE: GO TO BEDROOM AND LOCK DOOR.

The first instruction in Operation Groove was already a no-go. I didn't have a lock on my door. As if my parents would have let me have a lock on my door. Instead, I closed the door and quietly placed my chair in front of it.

STEP TWO: OPEN CURTAINS AND BLINDS.

That was easy. I pulled the brown and cream floral curtains apart.

STEP THREE: TURN ON ALL LIGHT SOURCES.

I switched on my bedside lamp and the main light.

STEP FOUR: ATTACH WALKMAN TO BODY AND PLAY FAVOURITE CD.

My favourite CD was already in my walkman so I put on the headphones and pressed 'play'.

STEP FIVE: JUMP AND DANCE AROUND YOUR BEDROOM, NOTICING THE DIFFERENT MOVES AND STYLES YOU CAN DO IN THE REFLECTION OF YOUR BEDROOM WINDOW. IT WILL NEED TO BE DARK OUTSIDE TO SEE A REFLECTION.

Tea Service's number one song, 'Delighted' boomed into my headphones. I watched my reflection as I leapt around the room.

STEP SIX: TAKE NOTE THAT NO-ONE CAN SEE OR HEAR YOU. YOU CAN DO ANY DANCE MOVE YOU WANT. NO-ONE IS THERE TO LAUGH AT YOU OR CALL YOU AN UNCO.

I began swinging my arms around and doing ballet jumps across the room. I wiggled my backside and made large circles in the air with my hands. My reflection told me I still looked like a dork, but I didn't care. I was having fun! The best part of the song came on so I jumped on my bed and danced away. Soon I realised that the girl in the window was actually looking like a pretty good dancer. I was astounded. Louie's Operation Groove had worked. She'd got me dancing without looking like a dork. The key was not worrying about what other people thought of you. I moved with the music and quietly sung along with the chorus.

'Peppermint tea for thee?
Delighted, I say.
Why can't she see
The problem my way?
Will it always be like this?

Ending in an angry kiss.
Delighted. Delighted. Delighted.
Delighted. Delighted. Deliiighted.'

I took a huge leap off the bed and landed in a rock star pose in front of the window. Then I pretended I was one of the pretty girls dancing around in the background of Tea Service's video clip.

Suddenly, there was a tap on my shoulder. I screamed and threw the headphones off.

'Dad!' I was horrified. Dad was in my room. How had he got in without me noticing? How long had he been standing there? Had he seen me dancing around my bedroom? My face was burning hot and I knew it was bright red.

Dad stood there, awkwardly. 'I did knock but you obviously couldn't hear me.'

'Hmm, sorry,' I mumbled.

'Your mother and I heard a commotion coming from your room and we were worried that something was wrong.'

'I'm fine.'

'So it seems . . . well, yes, um . . .' Dad looked just as embarrassed as I was. 'Um, I'm off to catch my plane for the conference down south. Just thought I'd come in and say goodbye.' Dad gave me a hug. I'd almost forgotten that Dad was going away for a whole week.

'Oh, OK, have fun.'

'Hope so. I'll be off then.' Dad looked like he couldn't wait to get out of my room. As he lunged for the door, his embarrassment at seeing his thirteen-year-old dancing around her room was forgotten and his role as responsible dad returned. 'Why was there a chair blocking the doorway, Madeline? If there's a fire or some other catastrophe, you need to have clear exits out of the house. I don't want to see that again, understand?' I nodded obediently. He gave a wave and closed the door after him.

I slumped down onto my bed and covered my face with a pillow. How embarrassing!

'Madeline?' Mum said, as she knocked on my door.

'Yes?'

'Can I come in?'

I prayed that Dad had not told her I was dancing around my room.

'Yep.'

'I thought I'd pop my head in to remind you we have to be at the dentist for nine. You hadn't forgotten, had you?'

As if.

'Nope.'

'Oh, good. So, you're dressed and ready to go, Dad said.' It seemed like he had told her. I felt my face go red again. This was so humiliating. 'OK, well I'll leave you alone then, shall I?'

I nodded eagerly. I was going to kill Louie. She knew I didn't have a lock on my door. Operation Groove was way too risky to attempt without that vital piece of equipment.

Our car passed only three teenagers with braces or plates as we drove to the dentist's. Only three kids out of about fifty.

'Mum, do I really have to get a plate? My teeth aren't that bad,' I pleaded.

'Madeline, you are very lucky to have the chance to fix those teeth up before it's too late. You don't want to find yourself with a set of fake ones like your Nan has, do you?'

'Hmm. It was true. I definitely didn't want to have gross fake teeth like Nana Hazel. They often slipped out when she was eating. It was way more uncool than a plate.

'Remember that time when her teeth fell out into Dad's birthday cake last year?' I giggled.

'Oh, wasn't that terrible. And your poor dad had to search around in the cream to find them. Dad's cake was a complete mess after that,' said Mum.

'And remember the time she came to one of my drama school performances and couldn't speak properly because she forgot to bring her teeth?'

Mum burst out laughing. 'That's right! No-one could understand a thing she said.' Mum tried very hard to wipe the grin off her face. 'Actually, Maddy, we shouldn't laugh about your poor nana's teeth. We'll all be old one day, won't we?'

Several old people just happened to be entering my dentist's clinic as we pulled up. I wondered how many were going in for false teeth. Maybe a plate wasn't that much of a tragedy.

In the waiting room, I collected the teen magazines and searched through them to see if there were any photos of my beautiful, tall friend, Dene. Deno sometimes models as well as acts, so she's often in magazines wearing chic clothes. I love seeing the stuff she gets to wear. I methodically scanned every page in each magazine but she didn't seem to be in any of them. I dumped them on a small table next to my chair and looked around the room at the other victims waiting to have teeth ripped out, drilled into, replaced or cleaned. I wondered if anyone was petrified. Statistics say that more people are petrified of going to the dentist than nearly anything else. Louie's dad is so scared that he hasn't been since he was fifteen. Several old people sat waiting (one of whom didn't look petrified at all; he was picking his nose; gross!) as well as two other teenage girls (who looked about as excited as me) and a very stylish woman wearing the most incredible black knee-high boots I'd ever seen. Meano Deno and the girls would go crazy over them. We love high-heel boots. It was the one piece of clothing that we all agreed was funky. The stylish woman pushed her sunglasses up onto her head and to my surprise, I realised that it was Wendy DeCarle, the famous singing teacher.

Mum spotted her too. 'Darling, isn't that the teacher you did a workshop with?' she whispered.

'Yeah, she's an incredible singer, Mum.'

'I should hope so after what she charged,' Mum said out of the corner of her mouth.

'Mum! She's the best teacher in the whole country. It was worth it. Just having her name on my CV has got me so many singing jobs. I think I've already paid off her workshop from the last two jingles I did.'

Shelley, the head teacher at my drama school, helps me get jobs singing for commercials through her agency. As soon as I had Wendy's name on my CV (CV stands for Curriculum Vitae. I looked it up in the dictionary and it's a Latin phrase meaning what you have done in your life.) she instantly booked me two jobs. One was a song about a new soft drink and the second one was about kids being safe crossing the road. Both the companies use Wendy's voice all the time so when they saw that I'd been trained by her, I instantly got the jobs. Everyone in the music industry knows who Wendy DeCarle is.

I couldn't help but stare at the talented singer.

She was so well dressed. Every part of her was groomed to perfection. Her nails were expertly manicured in dark, plum-coloured nail polish and her make-up looked like she had just finished shooting the cover of *Vogue*. She had a dead straight fringe and her shoulder-length black hair was so straight I wondered if it was a wig.

I mouthed the word 'wig', at Mum. She casually tried to look over at Wendy, but she picked the exact moment Wendy was looking in our direction. Sprung!

'Oh, hello! My daughter was just about to come over and say hello. You're Wendy DeCarle, aren't you?' Mum babbled. I couldn't believe she'd dobbed me in to talk to Wendy. I was terrible at talking to people I didn't know that well and Mum knew it. The whole reason why my parents had agreed to send me to acting classes was because I was shy.

I noticed Mum's face was going red, like mine does when I'm embarrassed. 'Off you go, darling,' she said as she nudged me in Wendy's direction. I couldn't do anything else, of course.

I wandered over and sat next to her. I managed to put a big cheesy smile on my face. What on earth was I going to say to the best singing teacher in the country?

'Um, hello. I don't know if you remember me but I took an intensive singing workshop with you a couple of months ago. My name is Madeline Wilkinson.' I stared at her heavily made-up eyes in the hope that she'd remember me. But why would she? I was a loser dork, after all.

'Maddy! Of course I remember you. How lovely to see you again. Tell me everything you've been up to.'

I couldn't believe it. Not only did Wendy DeCarle remember me, she was genuinely interested in the work I'd been doing.

'I'm still taking my acting classes at the drama school I go to, The Shooting Stars, and not long ago I had a guest role in the TV show 'Halfway Hospital'. Um, what else have I been doing? Oh, I shot a student film up in the mountains, performed *Saint Joan*, the play, and at the moment, we are working on a shortened version of the musical *Grease*.'

Wendy seemed to be hanging on my every word. My life in the entertainment world surely couldn't be that interesting to her. She worked with musical theatre stars like Nathan Lane, Ute Lemper and Hugh Jackman.

'Maddy, believe it or not, you may have just cured the biggest headache I've had for the past two weeks.' I looked at her, confused. 'Let me ask you one question: have you ever heard of a band called Tea Service?'

chapter three

I tried to imagine my fluorescent bicycle outfit was actually a bright yellow fitted raincoat that Dene had modelled in a recent Calvin Klein parade. I wasn't going to let my hideous clown-like appearance force me to take the long way to The Shooting Stars again. I couldn't waste a single minute getting there.

I dumped my bike around the side of the building, quickly pulled off the jacket, helmet and pants, shoved them in my backpack and ran inside. As usual, my three friends were lounging around in the green room, being silly.

'No, *you* are my best friend!' yelled Dene to Louie.

'No! *You* are my best friend!' Louie yelled back.

'No! You are *both* my best friends!' screamed Tahnee.

I had no idea what they were doing and I didn't think it was wise to ask. Sometimes my friends' games had no meaning or logic behind them whatsoever. Instead I just blurted out what I had been dying to tell them all day.

'We are going to see Tea Service!' I yelled.

My friends stopped their strange game immediately.

'What?' asked Tahnee. 'What do you mean?'

Deno had already bounded off the couch and grabbed my hand. 'Are you serious? Did you say we are going to see Tea Service?'

They stared at me like I'd told them Elvis wasn't really dead. If I had been joking, they probably would have killed me.

'I'm serious. We are going to see Tea Service.'

'AAAAHHHHHHHHHHHHH!' The girls were screaming crazily. Deno pulled me into a hug and made us jump around the room.

From the roof came a loud banging. The younger kids were in their acting class upstairs and we were obviously disturbing them. Giggling, Louie put a finger to her mouth to tell us to shut up and pointed outside. We ran out of the green room, into the foyer, down the front steps of the building and onto the front lawn.

'AAAAAAAAAAAHHHHHHHHHHHH!' We screamed once we were safely outside.

'Coolio Schmoolio! This is totally five stars,' said Tahnee with glee. 'How in goddessness did you get us tickets? I sat up all night on the web trying to find some.'

The girls and I sat under a big willow tree and I explained the good news.

'OK. This is how it happened. I think it's

because I gave up the magic dice.'

Deno held her forehead with one hand. 'Oh, no. Not the stupid dice thing again.'

'No, you don't understand, I'm being serious,' I protested.

'Madds, you're always serious. We know you're being serious, that's what worries us,' teased Tahnee.

Louie told them off. 'Guys, let her tell the story.'

'Thanks, Louie. I have to tell you from start to finish otherwise it won't make any sense, OK?' The girls nodded. 'OK. I was at school and I overheard Nina Karter—'

'Nina's the most popular girl at Madds's school,' interrupted Louie.

'Yeah. And Nina was talking about her birthday party and she said her dad got her tickets for a Tea Service concert. She also said that I was a loser and so were several other girls in my class and that's why she didn't invite us to go and see the band with her.'

Tahnee and Deno were looking confused already. 'Didn't you get my e-mail?' Louie asked them. The girls shook their heads.

'I only got one about trying to get Tea Service tickets,' said Tahnee.

'Argh! Our computer is always breaking,' complained Louie.

'Hang on a minute. This girl called you a loser? Who does she think she is?' said Deno angrily.

'Everyone stop interrupting. Let Madds finish her story,' berated Tahnee.

'Anyway, I was furious that Nina said I was a loser and so I decided to kind of get my act into gear. I decided to stop playing maths games like the magic dice, because everyone seems to think it's dorky—'

'It is dorky,' butted in Dene.

'Deno!' yelled Lou and Tahnee.

'Sorry. Carry on, Madds.'

'I'm also no longer going to wear my fluorescent outfit when riding my bike. Dad's away at the moment, but as soon as he gets home I'm going to tell him that I refuse to wear it anymore.'

'There is no way that you are going to tell your dad you're not wearing that thing. No way!' said Dene.

'Deno!' warned Louie.

'I am going to tell him. I've decided. And I've managed to convince Mum to pay a little bit extra for a hidden plate instead of those ones where you can see the wires and stuff.'

'I'm sorry, Queen Tahnee and Princess Lou, for interrupting again, but I still have no idea what any of this has got to do with Tea Service tickets,' Deno protested.

Louie turned to me with a shrug. 'Sorry,

Madds, but I kind of agree. What does this have to do with Tea Service tickets?'

'I was about to get to that. When I was in the dentist's waiting room, I bumped into a famous singing teacher I've taken some classes with. It just so happens that she is one of the organisers of this year's Helping Hands Heart-warming Telethon. And guess who the big celebrity guest is this year?'

'Tea Service!' my friends squealed.

'So you managed to get us tickets to the telethon? That's incredible. You are the best, Madds.' Tahnee jumped on me and gave me a big hug.

'No! It's better than that, guys. I didn't get us tickets to the telethon, I got us *in* the telethon, performing with Tea Service!'

There was silence.

'Performing as what?' asked Lou.

'As their back-up dancers and singers,' I quickly muttered. I knew this was going to be the hurdle I had to get my friends over. Once they got over having to sing and dance on national TV, they would realise how exciting it was to meet Tea Service. Although the dumbstruck look on their faces was not very encouraging. I gave the girls a big smile. No-one smiled back. This was going to be a lot tougher than I thought.

'Did she say we are going to be their back-up dancers and singers?' Deno asked. Louie and

Tahnee nodded. 'I'm sorry, but I didn't know I could sing. I should put that on my résumé. Why hasn't anyone told me I'm blessed with this gift?'

I took a deep breath. The girls didn't seem to be reacting too well to the news. Tahnee and Lou were quiet as mice and Deno was glaring angrily at me.

'Look, guys, we may not be the best musical performers in the whole world but it's only backing up a pop band. I'm sure we can fudge our way through it.' The girls looked very unsure. 'It's only a pop band. It's not like we have to perform opera or something.' My friends were still dead silent. 'Guys! You get to meet Tea Service in person!'

It was time to go into our lesson so we headed for the classroom on the top floor.

'I don't know about this, Madds. You're saying we have to sing and dance, right?' Louie asked.

'Yeah, that's all.'

'That's all,' Deno interrupted. 'I hate to point it out to you, but I can't sing.'

'That's OK, Dene Runga, I can't dance. I'm still going to have a great time meeting Tea Service.'

'What sort of dancing do we have to do?' asked Tahnee, as we climbed the wooden staircase.

'I'm not really sure. They'll show us in rehearsals.'

'Well, I'd really like to meet Tea Service, but

I'm not sure if I want to go on TV and make a fool out of myself,' said Louie. 'I'll have a think about it and get back to you. What's the latest we can tell you if we're in or not?'

'There is no latest,' I answered.

'No latest? Not a time? What do you mean?' she asked.

'Well, I've already said we'll do it. We start rehearsals tomorrow.' I timed my final comment well. As the words left my mouth, I leapt into the safe boundaries of meditation time at The Shooting Stars. You are not allowed to talk once you enter the classroom. I grabbed a lavender eye-pillow from the cupboard and found a place on the old Persian rug to meditate.

Louie, Tahnee and Dene were still standing in the doorway, dumbfounded. Shelley, our teacher, motioned for them to come in and shut the door. My friends were still firing laser glares my way, so I quickly lay down, placed the eye-pillow on my face and tried to think of ways to convince them it was a great idea.

Meditation seemed to go very quickly. Shelley talked about swaying in hammocks and walking through a lush garden full of every kind of flower you'd ever seen. My racing mind had me swing so fast in the hammock that I fell out, and there were so many different types of flowers in the garden that they looked like one big mess of weeds. She was distracting me from thinking about how to convince my friends to perform in the telethon. And I had to. When Nina Karter and her clones saw me dancing and singing with Tea Service, I would be treated like a princess for the rest of my school life; I was sure of it.

'OK, thespians, take as long as you need, and then slowly open your eyes and sit up. If you feel a little dizzy, lie back down again for a minute or so,' said Shelley softly.

The class slowly began to stir. Most of the kids were yawning and stretching, but my three best friends were looking extremely grumpy and flustered.

'Now that you are all awake, let's get right into some vocal warm-ups. I want you all to stand in a circle and, one person at a time, you are going to make a long ahhh sound while imagining the sound coming out of your mouth is actually a stream of coloured mist. For example, AHHHHHHHHH,' Shelley demonstrated. 'The colour I imagined was bright aqua. Now, everyone get in a circle and we will start the exercise with Samantha.'

Each kid made their sound and then had to explain which colour they chose. Sometimes you could almost guess which colours the sounds were. The people who made really high pitched 'aahhhhs' were often thinking of the colour yellow and the deep, resonant 'ahhhs' were usually dark browns or blacks.

Next, Shelley separated the girls and the boys to rehearse our songs for our performance of *Grease*. While Shelley took the boys to practise at the piano, the girls had to rehearse the three dances we'd learnt the previous week.

'Maddy!' growled Louie, once the girls in the class had assembled at the end of the room. 'I can't believe you told this woman we are going to do it. Why on earth would she take your word for it that we can sing and dance?'

'Because she's heard me sing and knows what level I'm at and assumes that you guys will be too. I told her we were doing *Grease* here at Shelley's so she thinks we go to a musical theatre school, not an acting school.'

Tahnee shook her red curls in dismay. 'I can't believe this. It's going to be a complete disaster.'

'No, it won't! I've worked everything out,' I tried to reassure them. 'I'll teach you guys the singing bits and Deno will teach us the dancing bits. It really isn't going to be that hard. You guys are stressing over nothing. It's just a telethon, it's not *The Phantom of the Opera*. You are going to get an opportunity that any girl in the country would kill for. And we get to stay at the ritzy Charlesworth Hotel while the telethon is on.'

'No way! The Charlesworth? I've always

wanted to stay there,' gushed Louie. 'That's the really modern hotel in the city. I think it might even be five-star.'

'Of course it's five stars. It'll be great,' said Tahnee.

'No, redhead. I didn't mean five stars as in it's the greatest, I meant five-star as in the rating they give to hotels to tell you what standard they are. The Charlesworth is one of the best in the country.'

'Absolutely fabulous, darlings!' Tahnee said in her posh, snobby socialite voice.

There seemed to be no more complaints from my friends once they knew we were going to stay in The Charlesworth. Hopefully, it was enough to convince them; I crossed my fingers behind my back.

'Rehearsals start tomorrow. I propose we have an emergency slumber party after them to practise some more, and hopefully, by the Thursday rehearsals, we will have it down pat. What do you think?' Three nervous faces looked back at me. 'You get to meet the coolest band in the country, you get to stay in the swankiest hotel in town and you'll all be doing me a really big favour.'

Small smiles began to appear in the corners of my friends' mouths. They couldn't say no.

chapter four

'Hello, girls, what can I help you with?' asked the receptionist at the Channel Forty-one studios. The girls nudged me forward. They had decided that in case we stuffed up or got in trouble, I had to be the spokesperson. They were the terms and conditions that Louie had clearly explained to me in her snooty-lawyer voice. I couldn't believe it. They were expecting me, the shy one, to talk us through this tricky situation? Had my friends gone mad?

'My name is Maddy Wilkinson and we are here to work on the telethon,' I said nervously.

To my relief, the receptionist, who's name tag read Jane, smiled warmly.

'Wonderful. It's great to have you on board. Who is the person you're after?'

'Wendy DeCarle,' I said.

Jane punched in some buttons on her phone and paged Wendy.

'I'm not sure how long Wendy will be. She's very busy at the moment. It might be wise if you girls go and take a seat in the green room. Go down that corridor and turn right at the end. It's the first door on your left.'

I thanked Jane and we headed for the green room.

'Unreal! We get to see another green room. I wonder what's going to be in this one?' asked Louie.

'Probably not a lot,' said Tahnee as she skipped along doing silly dances. 'This is a charity event, so they won't have a lot of money to throw around on things like food and snacks.'

Boy, was Tahnee wrong. We entered the huge luxurious room that was filled with tables of yummy snacks. Several people were lounging around munching them.

'Oh-o. I really picked the wrong time to become a vegetarian, huh?' said Tahnee, eyeing off a plate of sausage rolls. 'Yum!'

'You're becoming a vego?' asked Dene.

'Yeah. Mum finally convinced me. She told me to go to a couple of websites about animal rights and boy, are there a lot of horrible things happening to animals. There is no way I am going to contribute to the torture by eating meat anymore. That sausage roll was probably a baby seal once.'

'Tahnee!' the rest of us yelled.

> *'Baby seal, baby seal,*
> *Now wrapped in pastry,*
> *How horrible does it feel*
> *When humans act so hasty?*
> *Should a tasty snack,*
> *Be all that you're here for?*

Baby seal, baby seal,
I'll eat you no more!'

'Tahnee!' we screamed. She truly was crazy.

A lady in a white apron walked past us with a steaming dish. 'If anyone would like some bolognaise lasagne with triple cheese, it will be waiting for your consumption in the dining room,' she announced to the room.

Several people sitting around took her advice and got up and headed for the dining room. A man in his early twenties, who I thought I recognised as the host of 'Quizz Whizz', a kid's game show, got up and went too.

'You girls coming? Mildred makes the best lasagne on the planet,' he said with a grin, and hurried out.

Louie began searching around in her bag.

'Great,' said Tahnee. 'This is going to be torture. Not only am I going to make a fool of myself on national television, but now I'm going to have my decision to be a vegetarian rubbed in my face.'

Deno giggled. 'You are such a drama queen, Tahnsta. If you are so desperate to have some lasagne, just eat it. No-one cares but you.'

'That's not true, Deno,' announced Louie. 'I care. I think it's great that Tahnee has taken this step and I think we should help her stick to it.'

'Oh really, Pooey.'

'Really. In fact I have a great idea how to help her. I'll go and eat her serving of lasagne!'

Tahnee rolled her eyes. 'Thanks, Pooey. You're the best.' Tahnee pretended to punch Louie.

'Guys, we can't go off and eat lasagne. We have to wait here for Wendy DeCarle. We have work to do, remember?'

'I'm trying not to, but you just reminded me. Thanks for that.'

I poked my tongue out at Deno. If the girls kept behaving like this, I'd go mad.

'Hey, goddesses, think we'll see some celebrities today?' asked Louie.

'Of course we will, Pooey. It's a telethon. They're full of celebrities. That's the whole point,' teased Deno.

'Look! There's one now,' whispered Tahnee. Walking down the corridor was Fred Nailor, the lead actor from 'Sharp Shards', a new cop show. We couldn't help staring as he headed towards the green room. Louie rummaged in her bag again.

'What are you looking for?' I asked.

'This!' Louie pulled out a camera.

'What are you going to do with that?' I asked nervously.

'Er, der. What do you think, Madds? She's going to take pictures,' said Tahnee.

'You can't!' I said in horror. 'That really would not be a cool thing to do, Louise Eary. Wendy thinks we are professionals who will fit into the telethon like old hands. You can't go round taking photos of people and stressing them out. We're not supposed to be fans who have snuck in, we're supposed to be professional back-up dancers.' My eyes pleaded with Louie as Fred got closer and closer to entering the green room. I prayed that she would not ruin the whole thing by taking a photo. I was sure we'd get kicked out if she did.

'Hi, girls,' Fred said as he walked in and headed over to the fridge. 'What are you four doing in the telethon?'

Dene stood up and shook his hand. 'We're the back-up performers for the band Tea Service.' She was so brave!

'Nice. I'm Fred. I'm introducing a couple of segments and going on the panel. Maybe I'll see you in there?' he said as he headed back out.

'Deno! I can't believe you shook his hand. You are such a flirt,' said Tahnee. 'Wish I'd thought of it,' she giggled.

Louie threw me a very grumpy look. My best friend was not happy. 'Madds, I had everything planned. I was going to get tons of photos of celebs and write my very first article for our local paper. If I can't take photos, I won't get my story published. You know I've been wanting to start writing for ages.' Louie put on this sad puppy dog kind of face. 'This is my big chance, Madds.'

Thankfully, Wendy DeCarle came in and saved me from having to deal with a sulking Louie.

'Hi, Maddy! These must be your friends.' Wendy shook each of the girls' hands and introduced herself. 'As you can imagine, I'll be running around like a headless chook for the next few days, so I'll have to throw you right in the deep end.' My friends' eyes grew wide with fear. 'I'll take you into a rehearsal room and Martin, our choreographer, will go through the routine with you.'

We grabbed our bags and followed Wendy along the corridors. I could hear the girls giggling and whispering to each other as we passed more celebrities. I crossed my fingers and hoped that Louie had left her camera in her bag and Deno wasn't shaking too many people's hands. I had a feeling the can of worms I'd forced open was actually a truck full of elephants.

'In here, girls.' Wendy ushered us into a small room that had mirrors for walls. A man sat on the floor, stretching. 'This is Martin. Martin, these are our back-up dancers for Tea Service. I'll leave you to it,' she said and sailed off.

We were left with the very flexible Martin staring at us from under a leg.

'How is he doing that?' whispered Tahnee. 'He's like one of those rubbery bendy toys that you can twist in any direction,' she giggled.

'Hello, girls. I don't have a lot of time with

you, so I'll just show you your routine, you can rehearse it and that will be it. These telethons never give us much time, do they?' Martin had a foreign accent. It might have been Russian.

'Great. We've got Mikhail Barishnikov teaching us,' whispered Dene.

'Who's that?' Louie asked. The rest of us had no idea who Mikhail Barishnikov was.

Martin lined us up in front of one of the mirrored walls and showed us the routine he'd choreographed. It looked pretty hard, especially for an unco like myself. I tried to remember how I'd felt when I was doing Operation Groove.

'Now, you guys can copy. And five, six, seven, eight—'

To my relief, Martin was interrupted by a young girl at the door.

'Excuse me, Martin, but Katie Wall has fallen over in rehearsals and they need to speak to you about how to change her dance.'

'Oh, no!' Martin lamented. 'Sorry, girls, I'll have to go immediately. Poor Katie. What a tragedy! Carry on rehearsing and I'll be back soon.'

As Martin left the room, we sighed with relief.

'Well, I don't know about you three,' said Tahnee, 'but I have no idea what that man just showed us. It looked like a combination of tap dancing and ballroom. Deno, if you can't teach us how to do that before he gets back, he is going to discover what amateurs we really are.'

Louie and I turned and looked at Deno. She was the only chance we had. I really hadn't thought the telethon would come up with something so difficult. It seemed like you could never second-guess anything in the entertainment industry.

'Luckily for you three hopeless uncos, I can remember what he showed us. I can teach you how to do it, no probs.'

Deno spent the next fifteen minutes going through the dance with us individually. I was surprised at how nice and polite Deno was when she was talking about dance. Normally she'd be yelling and holding her head, but it seemed that when it came to dance, she was very calm and composed. It was a side of Deno I'd never seen.

Tahnee also noticed the change in our brash friend. 'Is there something wrong with you, Deno? You don't seem to be as rude as you normally are.'

'Shut-up, Redhead. Just concentrate on pointing your toe as you kick your leg up, OK?'

'That's more like it,' said Tahnee. Deno grabbed Tahnee's upright leg and began shoving it towards the ceiling.

'Ah!' screamed Tahnee. 'That hurts.'

'I know, that's why I'm doing it. Are you going to behave or are you going to keep hassling me?'

'Behave, behave, behave,' Tahnee pleaded.

Louie and I got the giggles.

'Now, let's go through the dance together. Remember, Maddy, to add in that extra turn at the start. You always forget it. Louie, don't do your turns too quickly. If one of us is out of sync, the whole thing will look ugly. And Redhead, don't be such a loudmouth and just concentrate on not falling off the stage. Here we go. Five, six, seven, eight,' she counted us in.

To my surprise, my amateur dancer friends actually looked pretty good. Even I didn't look like too much of a dork. Deno was a really good teacher. The girls and I danced and danced until we thought we were brilliant at the routine.

'Sorry about that, girls,' said Martin as he swanned back into the room. 'Now, let's see the end result of my creation. Five, six, seven, eight.' Martin clapped his hands to give us the beat.

Amazingly, we performed the dance in sync and with no stuff-ups.

'OK. It needs a little bit of work, but I'm sure you'll have it finessed by tomorrow. Darling, you are not quite in time with the others,' Martin told me. 'Sweetie, your leg kicks are really uncontrolled,' he said to Louie. 'And you, my friend,' he said turning to Tahnee, 'have to stop watching the others and stop improvising. I know this is only a telethon, but really, we don't have time to mess around in rehearsals. Professional dancers such as yourselves should know better.'

Before we knew it, Martin had rushed off to another rehearsal and left us standing there like dorks.

'He thinks we were messing around? He thinks we need a bit of finessing?' Tahnee said in fits of laughter. 'That guy has no idea!'

'That was the best dancing I've ever seen you guys do,' giggled Deno, 'and he thought it was terrible. We are in so much trouble.'

As bad as the situation seemed, Tahnee and Dene couldn't help but find it amusing.

Louie, on the other hand, looked like she was going to be sick. 'This is not funny, guys. How are we going to feel tomorrow when he sees that we are still just as pathetic as today? We are going to feel humiliated,' she said.

'Oh, get over it. It's just a telethon. It's not like we are getting paid or anything, are we, Madds?' asked Tahnee.

It was true. We weren't getting paid for it.

'If you can't do something properly, don't do it at all,' stated Louie.

'What do you mean, Pooey? You're the one who's using this to become a big reporter for the local paper. If it wasn't for my professionalism, none of you would have got through the dancing,' said Dene.

In my head I could see the elephants jumping out of the truck and trampling everything. What had I done? This was turning into a nightmare.

'Come on, guys, let's not fight. The thing we want to concentrate on is doing a good job to impress Tea Service. How cool is it going to be to perform with the hottest band on the charts? If we concentrate really hard, I know we are going to be fine,' I lied. I had to do something to get my friends to stop fighting. Soon I'd have one of them quitting and we would never meet Tea Service. How would I ever make Nina Karter see I was just as cool as she was?

Wendy DeCarle stuck her head around the door. 'Hi, girls. Martin said you were done, so I thought I'd take you over to the music room.'

We followed her back along the maze of corridors to another small room with a piano.

'Now for more humiliation,' muttered Louie.

Deno poked her and mouthed 'shut-up'.

'Stand around the piano, girls, and I'll demonstrate what you have to sing.'

I listened to the song carefully and deduced that the girls had little or no chance of fudging their way through. Wendy had put in some difficult harmonies. I knew instantly that the girls would not be able to follow it.

'OK, Louie, this is the part I want you to sing, it goes like this . . .'

Louie's eyes pleaded me for help. But there was nothing I could do. I just had to stand there and listen to her commit singing suicide.

with the non... ...band on the charts. If we conce...ate

'OK, emergency slumber party. Either you and Deno are going to give me some serious coaching tonight or I'm not going to rehearsals tomorrow,' grouched Louie as we grabbed our things from the green room.

'Fine with me,' said Deno. 'My only other choice is going home to a very grumpy mother. Grumpy Louie or grumpy mother?' she sang screechily. Tahnee joined in. 'Grumpy Louie, grumpy mother, grumpy Louie, grumpy mother,' they chimed.

Tahnee had done quite well with the singing, but Deno sounded like fingernails scraping down a blackboard. Louie wasn't much better, hence her panic attack.

'Why's your mum grumpy?' Tahnee asked Dene once they decided to quit singing their silly song.

'I broke her favourite vase. It's Italian hand-blown glass and it cost a fortune. Her sister brought it back from Venice.'

'Oh-o. Meano Deno is in big trouble-o,' sang Tahnee.

'Tell me about it. Mum always seems to be in a

bad mood these days and this is going to be the last straw. I'd much rather hide out at the Tree House than my place.'

We call Louie's house the Tree House as it's built around a gigantic oak tree. We love having slumber parties at Louie's and her parents are really cool, so it's never a problem to organise them.

So it was decided that the slumber party was definitely needed. I used the phone in the green room to see if it was OK with my mum. Unlike Louie's parents, mine are highly protective and wrap me in fluro clothing at every opportunity. I crossed my fingers and hoped that she'd say yes. I normally wasn't allowed to stay over at Lou's on a weeknight.

'Hi, Mum. We've just finished rehearsals, but we need a bit more practice, so the girls and I thought it would be a good idea to stay at Louie's and drill the routine. Is that OK with you?'

Mum was fine about it! When Dad's not home, she always seems to be less stressed about things.

'But, darling, I do think it would be wise to give your father a call at his hotel. He's phoned twice to see how you are and you've been out both times. He thinks you are running amok without him here. Can you do that for me?' she asked.

'I probably won't have time. We're going to have to practise practically all night,' I protested. The girls would think I was a real baby having to check in with my dad. My new cool status was not going to be convincing if I had to talk to Dad.

'Darling, call him from Louie's. Mrs Eary won't mind and I'm sure you can find five minutes in your busy schedule to phone your father. Or perhaps you can call him from home before bed time?'

Mum had got me. I had no choice but to embarrass myself at Louie's house.

We put on our jackets and Deno managed to grab as many leftover snacks from the green room as she could shove in her mouth. 'I can't believe we still haven't met Tea Service. When are we going to see them, Madds? It's the only reason any of us are here, you know,' she said through a mouthful of food.

'At tomorrow's rehearsals, I guess. I kind of thought we'd see them today, too.'

'It's probably a good thing we didn't,' said Louie. 'They would've thought we were total jerks and asked for new back-up performers.'

Three very tall girls walked in so we ceased our conversation. If anyone found out we weren't really dancers and singers, we were done for. The tall girls each grabbed a soda from the fridge.

'Hey, is that you, Dene?' asked one of them.

'Hey, V! How are you?' mumbled Dene through her mouthful of food.

'What are you doing here? I thought we were

the only models here,' asked a girl with red, afro hair and dark skin.

'Oh, I'm not working as a model. I'm here as one of Tea Service's back-up dancers and singers.'

'NO WAY!' the three girls squealed.

'That is so exciting!' the one with the red afro said. 'We've been searching the place to catch a glimpse of them, but so far, nothing.'

'I didn't know you were a singer as well as a dancer,' said the prettiest one with straight black hair.

'Oh, yeah, I pretty much do everything. Singing, dancing, modelling, acting—'

'Lying,' said Tahnee under her breath. Louie and I tried not to laugh.

'Wow, Dene. That's so amazing. When you next see the band, make sure you come and find us so we can meet them, OK?'

The models waved goodbye as we left the green room. As soon as we were down the corridor, we broke into laughter.

'Oooh. Yes, I can do anything. I'm an acrobat, writer, surgeon, athlete, chef, computer technician,' teased Tahnee.

'Hey! I was just thinking of you guys. If I told them I couldn't really sing, it might've got back to Wendy and we'd be out of a job. I had to lie.'

'Yeah, right,' said Louie.

'OK, so it felt really good for my model friends

to see me cast as a singer and dancer. Now all I've got to do is learn how to sing.'

'Don't worry, Deno. After tonight's slumber party, you will be singing like Julie Andrews in *The Sound of Music*. Promise,' I assured her.

We were given a cab charge voucher and the four of us piled into the taxi waiting outside the studios. It wasn't long before we were at Louie's Tree House. Smoke was billowing from the chimneys and I wished that we could have a cosy night around the fireplace, but I knew that we would be working hard.

As we walked in the door, Louie's little brother, Jake, jumped around and gave us all hugs. He is so cute. I always wished I had a little brother like Jake.

Tahnee ran over to Louie's two furry Himalayan cats, Dizzy and Mozzie and began fussing over them. Tahnee isn't allowed a pet because she lives in an apartment with her mum. She goes nuts over Louie's cats.

'Hey, Mum, would it be all right to make tonight's dinner vegetarian? Tahnee's decided to try being a vego.'

'Not a problem. I'm sure I can come up with something mouth-watering.'

'Thanks, Mrs Eary,' Tahnee said with the sweetest smile you've ever seen. I tried not to giggle. Tahnee acts so differently around our parents. It's like watching a completely different person.

'How did the rehearsals go, girls? I haven't heard a thing about it since you came home.' We all looked at Louie. None of us wanted to tell her mum that we were hopeless and were probably going to make complete idiots out of ourselves just to meet a band.

'Really great. We just want to get in as much practice as possible,' Louie lied. 'So we might head up to my room and get started.'

'Fine. I'll get Jake to come and get you when dinner is ready.'

We ran up the spiral staircase that led to Louie's room on the top floor. Lou and Deno pushed Louie's bed to one side of the room and we rolled her rug up.

'OK. This should be enough rehearsal space. Let's start with the dancing.'

Deno went through all the moves again and then counted us in. We started to dance but, without the aid of the studio's big mirrors, she couldn't see if we were in time and who was getting what wrong.

'Hey! I've got an idea. What about Operation Groove?' I asked Louie.

'Great idea, Madds!' Louie jumped on her bed and pulled her curtains apart. But her stained glass window had too many different pieces of glass to form a good reflection of us.

'Now what do we do, you silly goo goos?' asked Tahnee.

'I guess you three will just have to dance and I'll watch and try and catch mistakes,' said Deno.

We must've gone through the dance a million times before Louie's mum called us down for dinner. Glumly, we plodded down the spiral staircase. It didn't seem that lots of practice was doing any good. We were still just as unco as we were at the studios.

Silently, my three friends and I ate our vegetarian lasagne and prayed. It was the only thing left to do. Once we were finished, we retreated to the lounge room.

'Come on, guys! It's really not that bad,' Tahnee said. 'Who is this Martin choreographer guy, anyway? He's probably some failed dancer who has to be a teacher. Who cares what he thinks of our dancing? I think we were great.'

'I wonder what he's done?' said Deno. 'You know what? I bet we could find out on the net.'

We raced into the Eary's study and turned on the computer. Deno typed in the search words, Martin Tchechkov and dancer. Several pages came up.

'Oh-o,' said Tahnee. We clicked on one.

```
Martin Tchechkov, lauded dancer and
choreographer, has been the creative
```

mind behind many a pop star's dancing career. He has choreographed for Madonna, Kylie Minogue, Jennifer Lopez and Britney Spears, just to mention a few.

He was trained at the Astrov Academy of Dance in Russia and has taken teaching positions in revered dance academies right across the world.

Martin has also won several awards for his performances in Swan Lake, Scheherazade and many of his own pieces.

Although trained as a classical dancer, it has been his modern choreography that has made his name famous in the world of dance.

'I can't believe it,' said Tahnee with her head in her hands. 'We are being choreographed by J Lo's dance teacher. I'm not sure if this is the worst thing that's ever happened to me, or the best. My brain is in complete civil war.' Tahnee put on two different voices to explain: 'Oh no, we have to be good because he's taught J Lo and Madonna.' 'Oh, my goddessness, he's taught J Lo and Madonna; this is the coolest thing in the whole world.'

Louie demanded that we head upstairs again for more practice. Her face had turned almost grey from stress. Louie hates being bad at things and she was determined that we would perform well in the telethon. After rehearsing the dance ten more times, she instructed me to go through the song again.

'OK, but I have to phone my dad, if that's OK, Lou,' I said.

She nodded and took me downstairs to their kitchen phone. Luckily Dad had to go off to a business dinner so I only had to talk to him for a few minutes. Like Louie, I lied about how things were going. Our parents would probably pull us out of the telethon if they knew we weren't up to it. Especially if they knew we were only doing it to meet pop stars. Finally when I got off the phone, Louie and I raced upstairs to start the singing practice.

We didn't have much to sing, it was just that the bit we had was difficult. All of us had to sing differently to produce a nice harmony, so it wasn't like we could copy each other.

'Remember, girls, do not listen to each other. Focus only on your part in the song.'

We were still singing late into the night.

Jake had been put to bed and was getting very annoyed with us. 'Shut-up!' he kept yelling from his room. Eventually he decided to come into Lou's room and tell us off. 'Can you be quiet? I'm trying to sleep.'

'Sorry, Jakeys. It's just that we have to sing this song tomorrow and we still aren't getting it right.'

'Yeah. I totally can't hit that note Wendy taught me.' Deno flopped onto Louie's bed in despair.

'How does it go?' asked Jake. 'Maybe I can hit it.' We all rolled our eyes.

'Really, Jakeys. You think you can sing Deno's part, huh?' asked Louie.

'I bet you I can,' he challenged.

Jake takes classes with The Shooting Stars young performers' group. Even though taking acting classes won't make you a singer (as my friends were showing), I decided to humour him.

'OK, Jake, this is how it goes: "Delighted, Delighted, Delighted. Ooohh-eeerrrr. Ooohh-eeeerrrr".'

Jake listened intently and then copied me. Exactly.

Deno sat up on the bed and stared in horror at him.

Jake began to giggle. 'Told you I could do it.'

'Get him!' yelled Louie. Tahnee, Louie and I lunged at Jake, dragged him to the bed and tickled him until his eyes were watering.

Deno sat on the edge of the bed, stunned.

chapter six

As soon as school finished, I had to leap in a taxi and head straight to the studios. I prayed that my three friends would be doing the same. From the look on Dene's face the night before, I had a horrible feeling that she might not turn up for the final rehearsal.

To my relief, they were waiting in the green room for me.

'I'm so glad that you're here,' I gushed. 'I was a bit worried you might not turn up.'

'I almost didn't turn up. But it was either make a fool of myself here and get to meet Tea Service, or go home to deal with Mum and the broken vase. Strangely enough, this option seemed better.'

'Your mum must really be stressed out if you're that scared of her,' said Louie.

'Maybe she's going through menopause,' offered Tahnee. We all looked at her.

'What's that?' Louie asked.

'I don't know, but every time my mum gets angry at my grandpa, he asks if she's going through menopause.'

'I think I'm going to go through menopause if we don't get through this rehearsal,' said Deno.

A woman reading a magazine in the green

room let out a loud laugh. 'I don't think so, darling,' she chuckled and flipped to the next page.

'Hello, girls!' Wendy bounded into the room and motioned for us to follow her. 'We are going to put you on set for a lighting check. The band is waiting.'

The blood rushed to my face as we headed down the corridor towards the studio door.

'This is so exciting!' whispered Deno.

'I brought my camera so I can get a shot of us with them,' Louie whispered to Dene.

'Louie! No,' I warned her. She pulled a face at me and put her camera back in its case.

Wendy pushed through the heavy studio doors and we walked onto a huge platform that looked kind of like a gigantic hand.

'What do you think?' she asked us.

'It looks like a hand,' said Deno.

'That's because it is! Oh, I'm so glad you could tell it was a hand. Several people thought it was a set of wonky piano keys.' She led us up to a dark platform up the back of the hand. 'Stand here, girls, and they will start lighting you. It'll take about twenty minutes.'

Wendy rushed off again and the four of us stood there nervously.

'B6!' yelled a man's faraway voice. A big green light illuminated us.

'No! That's not it. Try B9!' he yelled. An orange light came up on our faces. 'Yep! That's the one, Harry.'

The orange light pierced our eyes and made us squint. But even so, I could still make out the spiky hairstyles of four boys, standing a few metres below us, on the middle of the gigantic hand.

'Look!' I whispered. We peered through the orange light to get a better glimpse of our favourite band standing right below us!

'Hello, up there!' yelled one of the boys. All of us were silent. What were we supposed to say?

'Hello, down there!' Tahnee eventually responded.

'Are you our back-ups?' another spiky-haired shadow asked us.

'Yep!' we yelled back.

'This lighting thing is a bit boring, isn't it?' the same shadow said.

'Not if you're good at shadow puppets,' said Tahnee. She made a rabbit on the white screen at the back of the studio, using the bright orange light hitting us.

The band gave her a loud round of applause.

'Impressive. But can you beat this?' asked one of them. He proceeded to make the shape of a dog walking on a lead. We returned the applause. These guys seemed really friendly and normal. Maybe they weren't the band. Maybe they were just stand-ins so the lighting guys could get everything right before the band arrived. Cool rock bands were supposed to be too busy and focused on their work to bother with a bunch of back-up dancers. Surely they didn't find shadow puppetry fun, either?

'Could you all stand one metre to the right!' yelled the faraway male voice. Everyone jumped to the right. 'Stay there and don't move. We should have this in the bag in a matter of minutes.'

The faraway voice was not lying. In a few minutes he had finished and told us to 'chill out' in the green room until it was time for the sound check. We headed towards the big green illuminated EXIT sign and into the corridor. We tried to walk as slowly as possible to see the band but they seemed to have disappeared.

'They probably have their own special dressing-room so that they don't have to deal with the general public,' suggested Louie.

Disappointed, we headed to the green room. The woman with the white apron was handing around mini quiche Lorraines to a few celebrities who were lounging about.

'Oh-no. My favourite,' said Tahnee. 'I love quiche Lorraine.'

'Have one, then!' demanded Deno who grabbed one and shoved it under Tahnee's nose.

'No, I can't. I'm determined to do this vego thing. At least for a week.'

'Are you a vego?' asked a voice behind us. We turned to discover that Tea Service was standing right behind us. Deno almost choked on the mouthful of quiche she'd taken.

'Um, y-yeah,' stuttered Tahnee. The boys were so cute!

'Me too!' said the lead singer, Nick Geoffries. 'How old are you guys?'

'Thirteen,' we all said at the same time. There was a pause. None of us knew what to say. We were so used to seeing them in video clips and magazines that it almost felt like you couldn't talk to them. They weren't real people; they were pop stars!

'I'm almost fourteen,' added Louie to break the silence. Deno shook her head in embarrassment.

'What? I *am* almost fourteen,' Louie said.

Nick picked up a bowl of rice crackers and pointed to the couches. 'Let's grab a seat, guys, before the cast of "Sharp Shards" come in. Those guys are like human vacuum cleaners. There's never any food left once they've been in here.'

The girls and I squashed together on one couch and the boys sat on one opposite us.

Matt Reeder, the bass player, started the small talk.

'We wondered if we'd even have back-ups. Apparently they had this big stuff-up and someone forgot to book them. How did they get you guys in at such late notice?'

'Madds was at the orthodontist and she bumped into Wendy.'

It was as if Deno had read my most feared

thought and decided to blurt it out. I stared at her in a daze, trying to look angrily in her direction, but I was so shocked and embarrassed that I just looked stunned. Of all the things she could tell the coolest band in the world about me, she told them I was a dorky teenager who had to go to the orthodontist.

'What are you getting done?' asked the drum player, Tony Hayes.

'Um, I'm, ah, um, I'm getting a plate,' I finally admitted. There was no point in lying. Anything I said, fillings, braces, false teeth, was going to sound equally as bad as a plate.

'Hey! Just like me,' said Matt.

'What do you mean?' asked Louie.

'I've got a plate too. I only got it last year. Bit of a late starter for getting my teeth fixed but better late than never, huh?'

It must have looked quite strange. I was sure my face was beaming with joy.

Now it was the girls' turn to look stunned. I guess none of us thought pop stars did normal, dorky things like go to the dentist.

'Is it annoying having a plate?' I finally asked after taking a very deep breath.

'Yeah, it is a bit. Especially when you are trying to perform. But, hey, it's going to be worth it in the end, right?'

'Yeah, I suppose so.'

This was so five stars! Not only were we meeting

the hottest band, they were really fun and interesting to hang out with, too.

Wendy DeCarle stuck her head around the door. 'Hey, guys. Just to let you know, we will be getting you in for a sound check in around fifteen. Cool?'

'Coolio, schmoolio,' said Alex Hilton, the keyboard player.

Tahnee sat there with her mouth wide open. 'Excuse me? Did you say coolio schmoolio?'

'Is there a problem with coolio schmoolio?' he asked in mock offence.

'I thought I was the only one who said coolio schmoolio.'

'Don't let this coincidence make you feel normal, Redhead, because I'm here to tell you that you're the biggest freak of nature I've ever met.'

Everyone giggled, while Tahnee and Dene poked each other in the ribs.

'Well, guys, they normally don't give us much time to rehearse, so do you want to go through the song out in the corridor?' suggested Nick. 'It might be worth getting a bit of extra practice in.'

My three friends turned to look at me. I was the spokesperson, after all. It was apparent that the guys in Tea Service were very professional and wanted to put on a really great performance. As soon as they heard us sing or saw us dance, we were in big trouble.

'Actually, we have a superstition that it's not

good to practise in front of the band before the live performance. A bit like the groom shouldn't see the bride in her dress before the wedding . . .'

Everyone was silent. I looked at the bemused faces before me. Had I gotten us out of it?

'OK, guys! Sound check time.' Wendy DeCarle had saved me.

The girls and I let the band walk in front of us so that we could plan what to do.

'I feel sick,' said Louie. 'We are about to make idiots out of ourselves in front of four really cute, famous and nice guys. We have to pull out, now.'

Tahnee and Dene looked equally worried.

'We've met them now. That's all we were really here for right? Let's take off and say we got locked in a storeroom for the whole weekend,' suggested Tahnee.

'You're crazy, Redhead. As if that would work,' said Deno.

'Shut up, Meano. You haven't come up with anything better.'

'Gosh, I hope I don't get dizzy, Louie,' I said to my friend. When I get overwhelmed, I sometimes faint. It's really embarrassing.

'You'll be OK, Madds. Take deep breaths.'

Before we knew it, we were standing up on stage. The big orange light warmed our faces and we could, once again, only just make out the band below us.

'OK, on the count of four, the intro music will start,' announced Wendy from the side of the stage. I was so worried, that I could feel my hands beginning to shake.

'Madds, what are we going to do?' Louie hissed.

I shook my head, helplessly. I had no idea. I felt vomitus as the first few bars of the song played. Suddenly, I thought of a solution.

I closed my eyes, let my knees go weak like we'd been taught in a movement class at drama school, and dropped to the floor.

I kept my eyes shut for a very long time and stayed still. It's quite amazing how hard it is to keep your eyes shut when someone tries to pick you up. Especially when it might be a total George pop star, like Nick Geoffries. But I knew I couldn't risk blowing my cover. I kept my eyes shut tightly and only began to open them when I was placed down on a soft surface, which I assumed was the green room couch. I pretended to groggily come to.

'Madds, are you OK?' Louie cooed.

I looked up to see the faces of Nick, Louie, Madds, Deno and Wendy, staring down at me.

'Darling, I think you might have passed out. How are you feeling now?' asked Wendy.

'OK,' I mumbled groggily.

'It was probably the hot lights, they often make people dizzy,' Nick suggested.

'No, it's just Madds. She's done it before,' said

Deno. 'She'll be fine after she's had a glass of water and a lie down.'

'No, no. I'll be OK to perform. It was just low blood sugar. I'll eat one of those biscuits and I'll be fine.' I took a chocolate biscuit from a plate sitting on the green room magazine table and began munching it with a smile.

Once we were in the corridor, I had my chance to explain Operation Technical Failure to the gang.

'Girls,' I whispered. 'I pretended to faint to stall until I could think of a plan.'

'Well done,' whispered Dene, impressed. 'I didn't think you had it in you, Madds.'

'So what's the plan?' Louie said urgently. 'We haven't got much time, we're almost there!' There was only one corridor to head down before we were back on stage.

'OK. When the music starts, Deno, you say your mike isn't working. Every time they check it or ask you to speak into it, just mime. Hopefully, they won't worry about it until tomorrow. They'll be more worried about what Tea Service sounds like. I'll sing louder to compensate for you.'

'What about our dancing?' asked Tahnee.

It was a good question and one I hadn't really come up with a good solution to. I put my maths cap on. Even though using maths was dorky, who cared? It worked for me . . .

'OK! Got it. The probability of Martin being

on set is almost zero. He seems to only be around the artists in the rehearsal rooms. In fact, the only time he seemed to go on set was if someone was hurt, right?'

The girls nodded.

'So, I calculate that he won't even be there. We can probably make up our own dance. One that's a lot easier than his.'

Deno clapped her hands in joy. 'That's great! We can do that dance we've been learning at drama school for *Grease*. We know that like the back of our hands, right?'

'Back of our hands! Good one, Deno!' guffawed Tahnee.

'What?'

'Back of our HANDS? The stage is a big hand?'

The three of us moaned at Tahnee's pathetic joke.

'Hey, one of us has to have a sense of humour in these trying times.'

It was agreed that Operation Technical Failure was to be put into action. Deno would mime and we would do our own dance, unless we spotted Martin in the audience. If he was, I had no idea what we would do.

'Chookers, guys,' I said as we walked back onto the hand.

'Chookers,' the girls replied.

chapter seven

Normally, I sat down the front in class at school.
Normally, I didn't care if it was considered a bit of a
dorky thing to do. It's a lot easier to hear what your
teacher is saying and it also means you have less
chance of being hassled by one of the tough kids at
school. But in Mrs Morrison's science class, I had
begun to sit up the back. A, because I determined to
become a cooler teenager, and B, because Mrs
Morrison's experiments often went wrong and I did
not want to die before I turned fourteen.

'Now, young adults, please note that you do
not put the blue liquid into the red liquid.
Otherwise, you will have yourselves a very big
explosion.'

I saw two kids down the front start moving
their chairs back away from Mrs Morrison.

'We put the blue into the beaker, then we put
the yellow into the beaker and—'

'No, Mrs Morrison! The yellow one, the yellow
one!' we all screamed. A huge bang interrupted us.
Several kids screamed and everyone ran to the back
of the room. Mrs Morrison stood behind her
Bunsen burner, her white lab coat covered in
chemicals.

'It's OK, young adults. I'm OK. Everyone calm down.'

'You put the red one in, Mrs Morrison,' Tod Landers explained to our stunned teacher.

'Oh.' Mrs Morrison looked down at the full vial of yellow liquid that was still sitting on the bench. 'So I did. Well, young adults, that's what you're not supposed to do,' she chuckled.

We stared at her in disbelief. Mrs Morrison really wasn't cut out to be a scientist.

'I'll go clean myself up. Talk quietly amongst yourselves about what you think would have happened had I put the yellow liquid in.'

'We would've actually learnt something,' whispered Tod.

The class sniggered.

Once Mrs Morrison left the room, I knew I had the perfect chance to do what I'd been dying to do all day: tell Nina Karter that I was going to be performing on TV with Tea Service. I hadn't said anything throughout the rehearsals, in case we got kicked out. If we had been, Nina would've said that I had made it all up.

Nina was sitting only a couple of chairs away from me, so I shuffled my seat over to her desk. I took a deep breath and quickly went over in my head what I'd planned to say. Deno, Louie and Tahnee had emphasised the need for kindness. Kill them with kindness, Deno had insisted.

'Nina, I just wanted to wish you a happy birthday for this weekend.'

Nina's face beamed at me. 'Oh, thanks, Maddy. That's so nice of you. I'm sorry you couldn't make it to my party. You're going to miss out on the best time.'

I was completely thrown. I couldn't make it to the party? She hadn't invited me to the party! What was she going on about?

'Nina, it's not that I couldn't make it, you didn't ask me to come,' I finally managed to say. How dare she make me feel like I'd turned her down?

'Oh, yeah, that's right. Well, either way, it's a pity, isn't it?' She was doing that smiley thing, but in her eyes there were evil daggers lunging out at me.

'No, it's not a pity,' I replied to her possessed face.

'Oh,' she looked a little taken aback. 'Why's that?'

'I couldn't tell you before as it was top secret, but I've been chosen to be one of Tea Service's back-up singers and dancers! Can you believe it? How great is that?' I gushed.

Nina did not move. Not a muscle in her face even twitched. 'You are not,' she said simply.

'Yes I am. I'm performing at the telethon. That's where your dad got you tickets to the band, right?'

Poor Nina looked like she was going to die.

'Maddy, you're lying aren't you? As if you'd be chosen as Tea Service's back-up singer!'

I felt my face go red, but this time it was from anger, not embarrassment. 'No, I am not lying. This weekend, my friends from drama school and I are supporting Tea Service. The organiser of the telethon is a singing teacher of mine.'

A few of Nina's friends were getting excited and whispering about how incredible it was. Yes! I was finally considered cool.

Nina noticed the commotion around her and put her hand up for silence. 'Guys, it's not true. It's just Maddy lying again. "Oooh, I'm a singer on the radio and I go to drama school and I've been in films and TV shows",' she mimicked me. 'Yeah, right! Maddy, you're a compulsive liar. Remember, girls, when I suspected she was a compulsive? Well, Maddy, you've confirmed it for us.' Nina pulled out the secret stash of lollies she always has hidden in her pencil case and offered them to all the girls except me.

There was no use arguing with her. Once Nina told everyone how something was, they believed her. But it didn't matter. I didn't have to prove it. The show that they were so excited to see would prove it for me.

Nina ate her candy slowly and threw me a nasty look. I looked down at my watch and calculated how many hours, minutes and seconds it would be until she would also be eating her words.

'That girl is obviously an idiot. I don't know why you are so intent on trying to be her friend, Madds,' Louie said as we drove past high-rise buildings in the city.

As soon as school had finished, I was supposed to catch a taxi to the hotel with Louie. Wendy had given us directions and a cab charge. But Mum had insisted on driving us there. She didn't feel very comfortable with me staying overnight in a big hotel and wanted to check that everything was legitimate and organised. Louie and I really wanted to catch the taxi but Mum wouldn't budge. It was either get in her car or not go to the telethon.

We sat in the back seat and gossiped while Mum nervously drove through the hectic city traffic.

'That's just it. I don't *want* to be her friend, I only want her to realise that I'm as good as her. If not better,' I explained.

'Hmm. That's fair enough,' said Louie. 'Hey, I've got a game for us. Let's pretend we are the ultra cool band, Tea Service, getting driven in our private limo to our sell-out concert. All the people on the streets are actually our adoring fans who are so desperate for a glimpse of us that they have lined the streets.' It sounded like a great idea but what would my mum think of it? She'd probably tell us to stop misbehaving. But it seemed that she was concentrating so hard on what roads to take that she didn't notice Louie rolling down the window and waving at some old guy.

I quickly rolled my window down too. Louie and I began waving at anyone we could see and yelled out rock star stuff like 'I love you too', and 'Thanks for the support!' Several pedestrians looked at us curiously and one even waved back! We were getting quite carried away with our role-play game, until we waved at a kid we actually knew.

'How embarrassing!' Louie squealed and sunk deep down in her seat. 'Do you think he recognised us?'

I was hunched down in my seat too. 'Hope not.'

'You girls really play some silly games sometimes,' Mum said. 'Ah, finally. The Charlesworth Hotel,' she said with a sigh of relief, as we pulled into the hotel's driveway. Louie and I lugged our backpacks out of the boot of the car, while Mum asked the doorman if she could leave it there for a couple of minutes while she checked out our rooms and whether our chaperone had arrived.

'I'm very sorry, madam, but this area needs to be clear for taxis and other guests' vehicles. I'll need you to park it over there in the car park if you plan on going into the hotel for longer than a minute.

What name are you booked under?' the doorman asked.

'Oh, I'm not actually staying here. My daughter and her friends are your guests, but I want to make sure everything is suitable.'

'I'm sorry, but if you're not a guest here, I won't even be able to let you put the vehicle in the car park.'

Louie and I looked at each other in dismay. This was so embarrassing.

'What company are the girls staying with here at The Charlesworth?' the doorman asked.

'The Helping Hands charity,' Louie said.

'Oh, how wonderful. Well, madam, there is no need to worry about your girls. The charity is wonderfully organised and always looks after the child performers extremely well. You don't need to worry about a thing if they are here working on the telethon. The chaperones are excellent and they even make sure the girls go to sleep on time!' he chuckled.

Louie pulled a face at me and mouthed the words 'child performers'. As if we looked like children. We were teenagers! It sounded like we weren't going to have any fun if the chaperones treated us like children.

'I see,' said Mum. She turned to Louie and me. 'It sounds like you should be OK. Madeline, you'll ring me straightaway if anything goes wrong, won't you?'

I nodded eagerly. It would be completely devastating if Mum walked us into the hotel.

'OK. Well, stay safe and have a nice time.' Mum gave both of us a hug and reluctantly got back into the car.

We waved goodbye and excitedly entered the grand Charlesworth Hotel. It used to be a very old-fashioned looking hotel but they had recently done it up and now it was funky and modern.

'How incredible is this?' asked Louie. In the middle of the foyer was a humungous ceramic fountain. Water spurted out of two cupids' mouths and lights changed the water's colour every couple of seconds. Above us the roof seemed a million miles away and everything was silver, black and grey. A man in a silver and black uniform took our backpacks and pointed us to the reception. I'd never stayed in a hotel like this and I had no idea what to do. Luckily, Louie took the lead.

'We are Louise Eary and Maddy Wilkinson, and we are here with the Helping Hands people.'

The receptionist nodded and looked us up on her computer.

'Welcome, Miss Eary and Miss Wilkinson. You two ladies will be staying in the Norton wing, which is on the first floor, and your room number is seventeen. I will need a signature from each of you to show that you have checked in. The telethon organisers will take care of the bill.'

We signed the pieces of paper and headed for the lift. It was made completely of glass so that you could see above you and out the sides as well.

'How beautiful is this? I love this place!' Louie exclaimed. 'Thanks so much for getting us into this, Madds. This has been the coolest thing we have done for a long time.'

'Don't thank me until we get through the telethon without making idiots of ourselves. Imagine that! When Nina sees me performing with her favourite band, I want her to be astounded, but what if we look like idiots and she ends up laughing at me? I'll be back to square one.' I thought for a moment. It would be even worse than that; I would never be able to go to school again.

'Maddy, that is not going to happen. We are not going to make idiots of ourselves because we are actors. If we can't actually sing and dance, then we will pretend to and we will pretend very well.' The lift stopped and we got out on the first floor. A sign pointed us to the Norton wing. Louie found the room and let us in.

'Wow!' we both said.

'Look at the TV!' screamed Louie. It was huge. It was bigger than my parents' bedroom window.

'Look at the stereo system,' I pointed.

'Look at the beds!' Louie jumped on a bed and I followed suit. They had to be the softest, cosiest beds I'd ever lain on.

'Look at the light!' Louie pointed to a strange silver triangle on the roof that had dozens of little holes emitting light.

'Look at the carpet!' I squealed. Beneath us we realised the floor was covered in a thick, cream carpet. It looked like polar bear fur.

'Take your shoes off,' instructed Louie. We kicked them off and stood on the luxurious, soft wool.

'Wow,' we both said.

'We know you are in there! Open up!' came an angry voice from outside the door. 'If you do not open this door in three seconds, we will kick it down!'

It was Tahnee doing her tough cop voice. I ran over to the door and unlocked it. Deno and Tahnee burst in.

'How cool is this place!' proclaimed Deno.

'This has to be the best place I have ever stayed in. Except that some strange man tried to steal my bags when I walked into the foyer. I must make a complaint about that,' said Tahnee.

I giggled. 'That's the doorman. He's supposed to take your bags.'

'Oh. I probably shouldn't have hit him then, should I?'

We laughed. Tahnee was crazy.

'So, guys, lets explore the hotel. Maybe we'll bump into Tea Service somewhere,' suggested Dene.

Louie and I put our shoes back on and locked our room. The three girls and I searched the stylish corridors, but there was no sign of the band. Deno and Tahnee insisted on going up and down in the lift several times and even decorating it with some plants we found on the ground floor.

As we walked along a section called the Wilde wing, we saw two maids urgently cleaning a huge room. One of them yelled at the other, 'Hurry up with those beds, Edwina. They're coming very soon! We want all of our guests to be impressed by our hotel, but Tea Service must think it is the most wonderful place they have ever stayed in. Bosses orders. Quickly, water the flowers on the coffee table and open the curtains. We have to get out. They'll be here any minute.'

The two maids finished their last chores and exited the room hastily. One of them had accidentally left a little chock in the door to keep it from closing. We looked at each other.

'Should we?' asked Tahnee. Everyone nodded. We couldn't resist. There seemed to be no-one in the corridor, so we quickly pushed Tea Service's door open and crept inside. Their hotel room wasn't just one room, like ours, it was three rooms! Each room had its own bathroom and the place was covered in bouquets of flowers from the telethon people, thanking them for performing.

'This is incredible,' said Tahnee. 'And I

thought our rooms were the best.'

From the corridor we could hear voices. Male voices. Voices that started singing.

'It's them!' I whispered. 'We've got to hide.' Deno pointed to the bathroom that was closest to the door. We ran inside and pulled the door shut just as the boys came in.

'Wicked. Take a look at this place,' we heard Nick's voice say. The boys 'oohd' and 'aahd' over their room. The voices seemed to be becoming fainter. They must have been exploring one of the other rooms.

'This is our only chance. Let's go,' Louie whispered.

We gently opened the bathroom door, checked that the boys couldn't see us, lunged for the front door and ran into the corridor.

'Run!' yelled Tahnee. We sprinted as fast as we could down the corridor to the lift.

'Hey!' we heard one of the boys yell.

'Quick,' said Deno. She had got to the lift first and was holding the door open for us. We piled in and she frantically hit the down button. We descended just as the boys reached the lift.

'We know you were in our room!' we heard Matt yelling.

As soon as the lift stopped at our floor, we leapt out and raced for our rooms.

'They could've gone down the stairs to catch

us, so keep running,' yelled Dene.

I don't think I had ever run so fast in my life. We reached Deno and Tahnee's room first. Deno unlocked the door and we ran inside.

'Think they saw us?' Louie asked once she'd caught her breath.

Tahnee was shaking her red curls. 'Nup. The lift left before they got there. We're safe.'

Suddenly, there was a knock at the door. The four of us froze.

'I'm not answering it,' said Tahnee.

'Me either!' I said.

'Me either!' said Louie.

Deno rolled her eyes. 'You guys are pathetic,' she walked over and looked in the spy hole. 'It's just a maid or something.'

Deno opened the door.

'Hi, my name is Marnie and I'm going to be your chaperone for the telethon. Can I come in?'

'Sure,' said Deno.

'Oh, great, you're all here! Hi, guys, I'm Marnie.'

We smiled and said hello to the pretty blonde woman.

'If you have any problems or you get lost while working on the telethon, come and see me,' she explained. 'I'll also be responsible for getting you guys to and from the telethon each day. I drive a blue Toyota, OK. So when I tell you to jump in my car, that's the one you look for. Sometimes I'll get you to grab a cab if I'm too busy.'

Marnie went through a few more instructions about the telethon and gave us each a running list of when we would be performing. Tahnee flicked through it quickly.

'It doesn't seem to say when we're on.'

Marnie took the schedule and read it.

'Oh, I see! Sorry, I completely forgot to tell you. As Tea Service is our biggest act, we are going to use the band as a device to have our viewers glued to their TV screens. We've come up with a competition where the viewers have to guess a donation amount that we have come up with to get the band to play. Of course we'll arrange it so that if no-one ever guesses the amount, we'll have them play anyway.'

'Does that mean we could be performing more than once?' asked Tahnee.

'That's right. We'll set an amount at the start of the telethon and as soon as someone guesses it, Tea Service will play. Then we'll come up with another amount, so the competition keeps going throughout the whole three days. It means you guys are going to be sitting in the green room a lot, as you could be asked to go on at any time. OK?'

Spending time stuck in the green room with Tea Service was totally fine with us.

'So, let's go, shall we?'

chapter eight

'Come on, just one teensy-weensy photograph.'

'No! It's not cool, Louise Eary.'

'I wish you'd give up on trying to be cool all the time, Madds. It's really not cool, you know,' joked Tahnee.

'Ha, ha! Good one, Tahnsta,' said Dene.

'Maddy, I'm here at this telethon as a favour to you,' Louie pleaded. 'The least you can do is let me take a couple of pictures.'

'No.'

Louie slumped down further on the green room couch.

Deno tried to console her. 'It's only the weatherman from the news, Lou. Do you really want a photo of him?'

'It's not for me. It's for my article in the paper.'

'Yeah, right,' teased Dene. 'You just want photos of celebs.'

Louie got up in a huff but very quickly sat back down when Tea Service walked in.

'Hey,' she said cheerily.

'Hi, girls,' said Nick. 'Ready to go?'

'Ready as we'll ever be,' replied Deno.

Marnie stuck her head in the doorway. 'Girls,

would you like to follow me to wardrobe?'

'Good luck, girls,' said Matt. 'Hope they don't dress you up in clown suits like they tried to do with us!'

We followed Marnie to the wardrobe room.

'I wonder what they'll dress us in,' said Tahnee. 'I hope they have my size.' Tahnee's really small and she often can't find clothes to fit.

In the wardrobe room, a girl named Andrea showed us our outfits. Black singlet tops and extremely baggy khaki trousers with huge red belts.

'I've also got you red sneakers to go with it. Try the outfits on, girls, and we'll make any adjustments on the spot.'

Our outfits were really cool. I'd never worn khaki pants before. Mum only ever lets me wear black and navy coloured pants because she thinks they are more 'wearable' or something. I looked at myself in the mirror. I looked cool for once! My singlet was a little bit loose, so Andrea put some pins in it and said she would take in the seam. Everyone else looked great too, except Tahnee's belt needed another hole because her waist was so small.

'That's an easy one,' said Andrea. 'We just get this hole puncher and, hey-presto, you have yourself a new belt hole.' The girls went into the make-up room while I waited for Andrea to re-sew my top.

'There you go.' I put it on in a little cubicle in the corner of the room. It fitted perfectly. I thanked her and went next door. A man named Aidan was inspecting my three friends' faces.

'You all look fine. This beautiful clear skin doesn't need too much make-up. Tiffany and Danielle, could you please put some light foundation on these girls, a bit of blush, mascara and lip gloss? Nice and simple.'

Tiffany and Danielle escorted Deno and Tahnee to make-up chairs and Louie and I sat down and waited our turn.

'So what's the plan?' Louie whispered to me. 'Are we going to do what we did last time? The *Grease* dance?'

'What else can we do? We're going to look like amateurs if we attempt Martin's dance,' I said.

'What about Deno singing out of tune?'

'We'll do the same. She'll have to mime. If they ask us to do a sound check she'll have to sing for that, but afterwards she can pretend.'

The thought of going on stage, with half the country watching, was beginning to make my stomach churn.

'Are you nervous, Lou?' I asked my best friend.

'Yep. I feel a bit sick. How about you?'

'Same.'

I calmed myself by thinking about how great it was going to feel when Nina Karter saw me perform with Tea Service. It was a great feeling, even though I was only imagining it.

Once Louie and I had our make-up done, we were sent back to the green room to hang out until we were needed on stage. When we got there, it was packed full of celebrities.

'Oh, my godessness,' said Louie.

Actors from all the shows on Channel Forty-one were everywhere. They were sipping cups of coffee and snacking on the delicious food. The hosts of 'Pet Care', this great show about animals, were there and so were a few of the newsreaders. Several sports people were wandering around, and a couple of pop stars.

'Is that Anita Jerry?' asked Louie.

'Anita Jerry? Where?' said Tahnee. Anita had this unreal song out that we were totally in love with.

'She's over there, see? In the pink dress.' Louie tried to casually point Tahnee in the right direction without Anita noticing.

'Oh, my godessness! I love her!' whispered Tahnee.

Wendy clapped her hands and got everyone's attention.

'Ladies and gentlemen, the telethon is about to start. Can we have all of our guests, except Tea Service, onto the stage for the opening number?'

The room cleared and the gang and I jumped on a couch. Tea Service was already chilling out on the other couch. Wendy turned a television on for us to watch the filming. We could see all the celebs getting into position. Music started and the lights slowly came up. Everyone on stage joined in on a song called 'Give us a Hand' that Wendy had written. When the song finished, the jam-packed audience cheered and clapped. John Dorset, one of the newsreaders, walked up to a microphone at the front of the stage and welcomed the crowd to the telethon.

The girls and I decided to make a hot drink while we waited to go on.

'Tea, coffee or hot chocolate?' Tahnee asked us as she bounded up to the drinks trolley.

'Hot Chocolate for me, Redhead,' said Deno.

'Dene Runga, you know you shouldn't have milky drinks before you have to sing,' I reminded her.

'Yes, I do know that Maddy, but I don't have to worry about that today, do I?'

'Why's that?' asked Alex from the band.

Deno froze. We were silent.

'Um, well, um, because I've begun having my hot chocolates without milk.' Dene looked unsure of herself and then babbled out, 'Tahnee becoming a vegetarian has inspired me to turn vegan and so I'm no longer having anything that comes from animals, like cows, you know . . .'

The boys burst into laughter. 'You can't have a hot chocolate without the milk!' said Nick. 'What are you going on about? That sounded very much to me like a big fat lie!'

Deno looked like she was trying to come up with another excuse, but it was no good. We had been sprung.

'You seem to be lost for words? Want to tell Nicky the real story? Why is our talented friend not worried about the cardinal sin of drinking milk before singing?'

'Actually, you're right, I was lying,' said Deno. Louie took a sharp breath in. Was Deno about to dob us in? 'You see, I'm actually having some surgery done on my throat next week and I'm not allowed to sing until it's over. But I knew Wendy needed four back-ups to make the dancing work so I told her I could come along for the dancing, and the singing I would just mime,' she lied. It was brilliant! The boys seemed to buy it.

'So, it's a hot chocolate for you, then?' asked Matt with a wink.

'Yep!' said Deno, with a charming smile.

'Why couldn't you tell us that in the first place? What was that stuff about being a vegan?' Alex asked.

The four of us froze again. Now what was Deno going to say?

'Oh, well, I didn't want you guys worrying about only having three back-up singers instead of four. Wendy said your voices are so good that you don't even need back-ups, but I know bands often worry about stuff like that.' Deno was a genius.

'Oh, right. I was beginning to think everyone

around here was mad. This afternoon we had some crazy fans sneak into our room. We couldn't believe it,' said Nick.

Deno had timed her first sip of hot chocolate very badly. She almost choked. 'Gosh, that's terrible,' she finally managed.

'Yeah, we don't know what they were doing,' said Tony. 'They were in there before we even arrived. I think they must have been hiding in the bathroom.'

None of us knew what to say. The girls and I pretended to be absorbed in the TV. We watched a panel of celebrities read out donations from viewers.

'Whoa, it looks like someone has already guessed the mystery donation number,' said the presenter. 'Congratulations, Erin Shipton from Haywood. It's time for a break, but when we return, we will have the much anticipated performance from TEA SERVICE!'

We could hear Marnie running down the corridor towards us.

'Guys! You're on,' she yelled. 'You've got about two minutes to set up. Let's go!'

We ran to the studio and took our places. As soon as the live audience caught a glimpse of the boys, they went crazy. I desperately wanted to look out for Nina Karter, but I had a bigger issue at hand. Making sure we didn't look like idiots.

'Sound check!' yelled some guys kneeling

beside the stage. 'Can each of you sing at performance level so the sound guys can adjust your mikes? We'll start with the band.'

The boys each sang the opening verse.

'We're on in ten, so we'll have to forget the girls' checks. And that's six, five, four, three, two, one!' The guy hidden beside the stage pointed at us to let us know we were on.

A loud voice-over introduced the band. 'Welcome back to the Helping Hands Heart-warming Telethon. And now, the moment you have all been waiting for . . . TEA SERVICE!'

The audience screamed and clapped as the band began to play. As if we were on autopilot, the girls and I began our dance and the singing without even thinking about it. We didn't have time to get nervous, it happened so quickly. And the lights were so blinding that we were mainly concentrating on trying to see where we were dancing. Before we knew it, the band had finished and the host of 'Pet Care' had begun to read out more donations. The guy beside the stage motioned for us to come off. He pointed to the stage door and mouthed, green room, to us. We quietly headed off while the celebrities read out viewers' names.

Once back inside the green room, we let out a cheer.

'Whoo hoo! Great gig, guys!' said an elated Matt.

'It happened so fast, I don't even feel like we performed the whole song,' said Nick.

'Yeah! That's how I felt too,' said Tahnee.

'It's weird. No matter how many performances we do, I still feel like it's the first one,' said Alex.

We all agreed. It seemed that being a pop star was a lot like being an actor. You always felt nervous before a performance, no matter how famous you were.

We sat back down on the couch and watched the telethon in progress. Soon it was time for Anita Jerry to sing. The girls and I watched closely.

An hour later, we were up on stage again. This time we felt a little more comfortable, and I managed to get a glimpse of the audience. But Nina Karter and her friends didn't seem to be there.

When we got off stage, I told Louie that I couldn't see Nina anywhere.

'Maybe she's got tickets for tomorrow's performance and not today's?' That had to be it.

We waited in the green room again, but Marnie was pretty sure that we wouldn't go on again.

'We don't want to wear out our best asset,' she explained with a wink. 'Even if someone guesses the next donation amount, we're not going to put you guys on. Feel free to get out of your costumes and I'll have someone drive you back to the hotel.'

The girls and I got changed in the studio's

toilets. We didn't have a dressing-room like Tea Service did.

'We did it!' squealed Louie.

'I can't believe we got through that,' said Tahnee. 'I was sure we'd stuff something up.'

Deno agreed. 'Yeah, how lucky were we that they didn't do a sound check on us?'

'And how lucky were we that you didn't blow the whole thing with your stupid poopid milk excuse in the green room?' teased Tahnee.

'Yeah!' Louie and I joined in.

Dene stood up for herself. 'I got out of it, didn't I?'

'Only just,' Tahnee giggled.

I sadly took off my funky clothes and put on my own dork outfit. I wondered if the wardrobe lady would let us keep the clothes when the telethon was over. I made a silent wish that she would.

We met Marnie out the front of the studios and she put us in a cab. 'I'll see you guys at dinner tonight, OK?' she said as we piled into the car.

Just as the taxi pulled out, Martin, the choreographer, came running out of the building. 'You girls!' we heard him yell.

'Drive!' squealed Tahnee. The cab sped off and we left a very angry dancing teacher standing in the middle of the road.

chapter nine

Saturday was spent hiding from Martin, the choreographer, and looking for Nina in the audience. On Saturday night, there was a big party for the entire telethon cast and crew, but Marnie only let us stay for an hour and then told us to go to bed.

We woke up bright and early Sunday morning to watch music video clips. Louie and I walked down to Dene and Tahnee's room and we huddled onto one bed together. The night before, Tahnee had said she would make us a special breakfast but I couldn't see any food anywhere.

'Where's this breakfast you promised us?' asked Louie. Deno and Tahnee giggled.

'You're sitting on it,' Tahnee explained.

Louie and I looked at each other. What were they talking about? Deno made us get off the bed and Tahnee pulled back the covers. A whole stack of red heart lollypops lay nestled in the sheets.

'Oh, my goddessness!' Louie grabbed the first heart she could reach. We all pounced on them and ripped off the clear wrappers.

Where on earth did you get all of this?' I asked.

'It iz top zecret,' Tahnee said in her German

soldier voice. 'I vould hef to kill you, if I told you, zo don't esk me egain!'

We got through two hearts each before it was time to travel to the studios for the final day of the telethon.

'What if Nina's dad didn't get her tickets? Maybe Tea Service is playing somewhere else and that is where Nina is going. If all of this has been for no reason, I'll die,' I whined.

Deno grabbed me and began shaking me up and down. 'Maddy! You are in this telethon because it is fun, it's helping underprivileged kids and you get to perform. You are not doing it to impress some snob princess from your school!' she growled. 'If I hear one more word about this Nina girl, I'll start singing instead of miming and get us kicked out, understand?'

Deno was joking, but I had the feeling she had no fear of exposing us for the fraudulent back-up performers that we were.

Marnie dropped us off at the studios and we cautiously crept inside. Luckily Martin was nowhere in sight. We headed to the green room and waited for the wardrobe people to call us in. Each day of the telethon, they had given us new outfits to wear. I wondered what we would wear today.

Tea Service walked in looking very tired and grumpy.

'Hey, girls,' Nick mumbled. 'Didn't see you

guys at the party last night. Where were you?'

'In bed,' I told them.

'Maddy!' My three friends yelled at me.

'What? We were. Marnie made us go to bed after dinner.' My friends glared at me.

'You guys must be smarter than we are, because we stayed out late and now I feel terrible,' said Tony.

I could faintly hear Marnie's voice in the distance.

'Martin, I'm sure the girls wouldn't have changed your dance.'

'I'm telling you, they did! I haven't worked with the best to have mere teenagers do whatever they like!'

'Quick, hide!' I whispered.

We jumped behind the couch that Tea Service had collapsed onto.

Tahnee stuck her head up and whispered to them, 'Please don't tell them we're in here, OK?'

The boys nodded.

'Hi, guys,' said Marnie to the band. 'You haven't seen your back-ups, have you?'

'No, man, we just got here,' said Matt.

'When you do see them, tell them Martin wants to have a word,' said the furious choreographer.

'Sure, not a problem. They're good, aren't they?' Nick said to him.

'What?'

'The girls, they're very talented, aren't they? I reckon they'd have to be the best back-ups we've ever had. Often we find the back-ups do some crazy dance that upstages us, but these guys are doing a really mellow routine. You've done a great job, Martin.'

Martin didn't know what to say. He made a big huffing noise and stormed out of the room. We waited behind the couch until Nick told us they had both gone.

'OK. Fess up! What have you guys done?' asked Matt.

We took our usual positions on the couch opposite them and spilled the beans.

Louie started. 'Maddy has this issue at school; no-one believes she is a performer.'

'She's a really talented singer and she's on the radio all the time singing jingles and stuff,' added Tahnee.

'And one day she bumped into Wendy who taught her in singing workshops. Wendy desperately needed back-ups for you guys and asked Maddy if she could dance as well as sing,' said Deno.

'And that day at school, this horrible girl who is the main one who doesn't believe I'm a performer, told me in front of everybody that I wasn't invited to her birthday party, to make me feel like a dork. Her party was getting to come and see you guys in concert and it was this weekend. So when Wendy asked if I could dance as well as sing, I said yes, so I could perform with you and make Nina feel like a total loser.'

'But Wendy didn't just need Maddy. She needed four girls, so she asked if Maddy had any friends at drama school who were professional singers and dancers. Maddy told her that we could do it,' explained Louie.

'I still don't see the problem,' said Alex.

'The problem is that only Maddy is a professional singer and Dene is the only professional dancer. We've pretty much had no idea what we've been doing the whole time,' said Tahnee.

'So when Martin, the famous choreographer, showed us the routine, we had to fudge our way through the rehearsals. We made a group decision that it was too hard for us to perform on stage without stuffing it up and looking like idiots, so we used a dance we learnt at drama school instead.'

'Hang on,' said Nick. 'You guys aren't really dancers and singers?'

'No,' we replied.

'We're actors,' I told him.

The boys started laughing.

I looked at the girls, confused. 'Why are they laughing?'

'Because it's so funny!' said Matt. 'You guys scammed your way into a telethon that you weren't capable of performing at and you've actually done a really good job!'

'No-one would know you weren't really singers and dancers. You guys were good. I didn't notice, did you?' Nick asked Alex.

Alex shook his head. 'I thought they were better than the last back-ups, that's for sure.'

'Hey, don't get too carried away. The only reason we seem good at the moment is because we don't let Deno sing. As soon as she opens her trap you'd realise we were fakes,' joked Tahnee.

'Redhead!' yelled Deno. 'Shut-up. I'm not that bad.'

Everyone was laughing by this stage.

'Are you girls in there?' came Martin's grumpy voice. We jumped behind the couch again.

'They're not here, Martin. We told you before,' said Tony.

'Have you seen them since I was last here?'

'No, mate. Not a glimpse.'

We heard Martin's footsteps stomp away.

'Thank you,' I said to the boys. 'He's really angry with us for changing his dance.'

'I don't know why. I thought your dance was really good,' said Alex.

'I still can't believe you guys have fudged your way into this whole thing. It's incredible. You must have an excellent acting coach,' said Nick.

'We do! Her name is Shelley and she used to be a really big movie star.'

'So, what sort of acting stuff do you guys do?' asked Matt.

The girls and I spent the next couple of hours telling them everything we had done and all our adventures.

'You were the girl in the butter ad where the cows dance?' Nick asked Louie.

'Yep.'

'No way! That's my favourite ad.'

'Deno was in a film a little while ago, but it hasn't come out yet, has it Dene?' Tahnee said.

'And Tahnee got on the news when she played a koala that—'

'Maddy!' Tahnee yelled at me.

'Oh, sorry.'

The boys looked at us for an explanation. We didn't have much choice but to tell them.

'You fell off the stage while trying to rip your koala head off?' screamed Matt with laughter. 'That's the funniest thing I've ever heard!'

Then the boys told us their funny stories about being in a band.

'Have you ever seen *The Blues Brothers* film?' Tony asked us. We nodded. 'You know the scene where they perform behind a wire fence to stop the audience hitting them with tomatoes and beer bottles? Well, we've performed in places like that.'

'Yeah, except the audience were smart enough to bring in small things that would get through the wire holes. Like peanuts. The whole gig, we were pelted with nuts,' said Matt.

Marnie walked into the green room. 'Girls, make-up is ready for you now and you boys can hit wardrobe. Oh, and Martin Tchechkov wants to speak to you girls about your dance.'

'Tell him that I made the change,' Nick said to her.

'You made the change?' she said dubiously.

'Yeah, what Martin came up with wasn't really grungy enough to match the band's image, so we asked the girls to do something a bit less arty and more teenage grunge.'

Marnie nodded with a smile. She knew Nick was lying, but she was obviously going to go along with it.

'Whatever,' she said with a giggle. 'These telethons are always so chaotic,' she added.

While we were in make-up, we got the call that someone had already guessed the mystery donation amount and we had to get on ASAP.

We ran into wardrobe, threw on our outfits, jeans and orange T-shirts, and raced to the wings. I tried to peer around the curtain so I could see if Nina was in the audience. If she wasn't in today, the last day of the telethon, all our hard work was for nothing.

A young actress from 'Sharp Shards' introduced the band and we ran on and took our places. The lights came on and the boys began. As I twirled around and sung my heart out, I had a couple of chances to look directly into the audience. Nina was sitting in the middle row! Yes! I moved as close to the front of the stage as I dared so she would see me. For one split second, I was sure she was looking straight at me.

The song finished and we raced off so that Anita Jerry could get up and perform.

'She was there!' I screamed to the girls once we were a fair way down the corridor. 'Nina was there! And she saw me, I'm sure of it!'

We only performed one more time for the telethon and then the boys got to go on for the finale number where the celebs sang the Helping Hands theme song, 'Give us a Hand'. All the back-up performers like us had to sit in the green room and watch it on the TV.

Martin had got fed up with looking for us and left to begin choreographing some famous singer's new clip.

'Oh, I bet it's Madonna or some icon like that,' said Louie.

'Imagine if Martin is complaining about us to Madonna! How funny would that be?' laughed Dene.

Once the celebrities had finished the song, the telethon credits rolled and the show was finished. Everyone piled into the green room to celebrate a successful end to a great weekend.

Wendy stood up on a chair to make a speech. 'Firstly, I would like to congratulate you all on such fantastic performances and contributions to this year's telethon. This is the most money we have ever raised so you must have been very entertaining!' The crowd cheered. 'But also, I would like to thank you dearly. When people aren't getting paid, it is often hard to get a good team together. But I think we have the best team I have ever worked with in this room, so thank you.'

Everyone clapped and one of the newsreaders made a toast to Wendy for organising the whole thing.

'And, before I get down off this chair, I'd just like to ask who raided the lollypop basket from last night's dinner. Some piggy grabbed nearly every heart and I didn't get any!'

Magically, my best red-headed friend was nowhere in sight.

'I think Tahnee might have gone to the toilet,' joked Louie.

'She's so crazy!' whispered Dene.

When the party started dying, Marnie gave us each a cab charge and a special telethon T-shirt to say thank you. We went around and said goodbye to all the people we'd met and made sure we got to say goodbye to the coolest band on earth, Tea Service.

I don't think I'd ever blushed so much in my life; the guys gave us each a hug goodbye! The other girls were going red too, even Deno. We grabbed our bags and took off before anyone noticed that we had turned into beetroots.

A cab was waiting out the front for us and Marnie waved us off.

'They hugged us! The coolest band in the world hugged us!' squealed Dene.

'I'm so embarrassed,' said Louie, holding her burning cheeks.

'Well, Madds, not only have you proved to Nina, the snob princess, how cool you are, you can also make her insanely jealous now that you've been hugged by Nick Geoffries!'

It was a great thought. I looked at my watch. Only fourteen hours and twenty-two minutes before Nina had to eat her words.

chapter ten

Mrs Morrison had obviously bleached her lab coat because I could only just make out faint purple splotches.

Nina had managed not to look at me all morning. Finally, Mrs Morrison asked us to try out an experiment, and so we could talk amongst ourselves and not get into trouble.

'Hey, Nina, have a good birthday?' I hinted.

'Yep, it was great,' was all she said.

I decided not to waste any more time. 'I saw you at the telethon, Nina.'

Her eyes seemed to glaze over and she pretended to be absorbed in the task of filling her beaker.

'You were in the middle row, right?' I added.

One of her friends, Stacey, looked at me in surprise. 'So it was you. I thought it was! Didn't I say to you, Nina that I thought it was Maddy dancing?'

All of Nina's friends began talking at once. They circled around me and asked a million questions about Tea Service.

'Girls!' Nina yelled. 'It was not Maddy. Can't you see she's lying again?'

'But, Nina, I'm pretty sure it was, and how else would Maddy know we were in the middle row?' Stacey asked.

Nina did her dagger trick at her. Stacey shut up and went back to her experiment. The other girls left too. I had a feeling that some of them knew it was me performing with Tea Service, but they were too scared to argue with the most popular girl in school.

I tried mentioning to a couple of girls what the guys in the band were like and how nice they were, but Nina cut me off.

'Maddy, shut-up! Can you stop embarrassing yourself for at least ten seconds? Everyone knows you didn't really meet Tea Service, OK, so just shut-up.'

No-one would meet my eye; they were pretending to be really interested in the stupid science project.

After everything I had gone through, Nina had still managed to make me feel like a dork.

I miserably went back to my own experiment and filled my beaker up with water. Mrs Morrison walked around and checked how everyone was going.

'Very good, Maddy. That looks like it is coming along very nicely. Oh, and I saw you in the paper this morning. So you're a big performer then? You students never cease to amaze me.'

'What paper?' I asked.

'You haven't seen it? Heavens above! You're famous, my dear. Michael, can you bring me that newspaper from my desk?'

One of the boys working down the front rummaged around on Mrs Morrison's desk and brought over a newspaper. The whole class was looking. Mrs Morrison found the page and held it up to show everyone, including Nina Karter.

Our teacher read: '"Local girl gives a helping hand. Madeline Wilkinson and her three friends, Louie Eary, Tahnee Caruso and Dene Runga, lent a helping hand at this year's entertainment extravaganza, designed to raise money for underprivileged children. The four girls performed with the chart-topping band Tea Service and said it was an honour to help raise money for such an important charity."' Mrs Morrison let out a heartfelt sigh. 'Isn't that wonderful? Well done, my dear. More of you people should help out with charities.'

'That was you performing with Tea Service?' said Michael. 'I thought it was, but you looked so different. What are they like?' he asked.

Stacey and some other girls crowded around me. 'I knew it was you, I just knew it!' She turned to Nina. 'See, Nina, I told you it was Maddy.'

Nina looked devastated. She had the exact same look on her face that I had often worn at school. The face that meant you just wished you could crawl into a hole and cover yourself with a nice big fluffy blanket. Now that Nina was standing in my shoes, it didn't feel nearly as satisfying as I thought it would. I couldn't stand the idea that someone else felt as bad as I often did at school. Even my worst enemy didn't deserve that.

'I guess it was hard to pick me out. The make-up people gave us really weird hairstyles and make-up,' I said to her.

Nina gave me a grateful smile. 'Yeah, I'd never seen you look like that, I guess.'

'OK, young adults, let's go through experiment number twenty-four, step by step,' Mrs Morrison announced.

Nina and I took our seats. I decided then and there that being nice was much more fun than being cool.

When school finished, I rode my bike home as fast as I could and immediately phoned Louie.

'Guess what! Guess what!' I squealed.

'Nina saw you in the telethon?' she asked.

'No! Well, yes, she did, but she pretended she didn't, but someone wrote an article about us and my teacher showed it to the whole class and Nina looked really stupid. Can you believe it? But then I kind of felt bad that she was upset and so I tried to make it into no big deal. Even though the kids were all much nicer to me, it didn't really count. Who wants friends who only like you if you're famous? And Louie, did you know there's a huge photo of us with the band in the paper—' I stopped short. 'LOUISE EARY! It was you! You wrote the article!' My best friend was giggling on the other end. 'I told you not to!'

'Maddy! If it wasn't for me, you couldn't have proved you were in the telethon, could you?'

It was true. Louie had saved the day.

'OK, it did help me but really, Lou, I could've got in trouble if anyone had found out that you were working as an undercover journalist. And what will Shelley say when she finds out?'

'Don't be so dramatic. It's only an article and anyway, I used a pseudonym.'

'What's that?'

'A fake name. I put the article under that instead of my own name. That way no-one knows it was me who wrote it. See, not a problem.'

'Well, I hope you didn't write any other articles or take any other photos.'

'Of course not.'

Out of the corner of my eye, it looked like Dene and Tahnee were staring up at me from a magazine on the kitchen bench. They were! It was a photo of them with the weatherman!

'LOUIE!'

Tempany
Deckert

attended a youth theatre
in Melbourne for six years
then hit New York
where she was trained
by some of the world's
best theatre actors.
Hanging out at Madonna's
parties in the famed
Kit Kat Club wasn't too
bad either! These
experiences have given
her plenty of material for
her new series,
The Shooting Stars.

Read other titles in The Shooting Stars series:

Number 1
The Green-eyed Monster

Those beautiful Cameron twins were *vomitus!* All the kids at
The Shooting Stars knew that. They were on TV all the time
and their oh-so-perfect faces were even on biscuit packets.

When the twins join The Shooting Stars, no-one wants to
know them. Then Louie goes to an audition with them and
finds out the *real* story behind their fairytale lives . . .

Number 2
Maddy's Big Break

When was Maddy going to get a *real* acting job? She was
always being asked to sing jingles for commercials. She'd
sung about chocolate, cereal and dog food. What if that was
all she ever did?

Then she got the good news in class: 'Maddy, you have an
audition for "Halfway Hospital".'

An audition! For television!
She just *had* to get the job.

Number 3
The Stage Kiss

Dene knows that being in a movie is going to be the best thing she's ever done, until she reads the script and finds out that she has to *kiss a boy*. She has never kissed a boy before.

Then she meets her co-star. Suddenly, everything's even scarier.

Number 4
Lights . . . Camera . . . Ghost!

No job could be better: the whole gang on location shooting a film in an old manor. The best setting for pranks, thinks mischievous Tahnee.

But weird things start to happen, things Tahnee knows she didn't do. What's going on?

Number 5
Understudy to Miss Perfect

There's going to be a summer school play at The Shooting Stars and Louie is *determined* to be the lead, Joan of Arc. She will even cut her hair and risk looking like a mushroom to get the part.

And get the part she does . . . but so does Kelly!
Who will be the understudy?